MW01657130

PRAISE FOR THE NOVELS OF KAREN FENECH

{GONE} Karen Fenech's GONE is a real page turner front to back. You won't be able to put this one down!" —NEW YORK TIMES BESTSELLING AUTHOR KAT MARTIN

{GONE} "Karen Fenech tells a taut tale with great characters and lots of twists. This is a writer you need to read." —USA TODAY BESTSELLING AUTHOR MAUREEN CHILD

{GONE} Readers will find themselves in the grip of GONE as this riveting tale plays out. GONE is a provocative thriller filled with a roller coaster ride that carries the suspense until the last page." —DEBORAH C. JACKSON, ROMANCE REVIEWS TODAY

{BETRAYAL} "An excellent read." —DONNA M. BROWN, ROMANTIC TIMES MAGAZINE

{IMPOSTER: The Protectors Series - Book One} "IMPOSTER is romantic suspense at its best!" —USA TODAY BESTSELLING AUTHOR MAUREEN CHILD

{UNHOLY ANGELS} "... a superbly intricate tale of greed, power, and murder... a suspenseful and believable story that will keep you reading into the wee hours of the morning. Highly recommended! —BESTSELLING AUTHOR D.B. HENSON

NOVELS BY KAREN FENECH

Betrayal

Gone

Unholy Angels

Imposter: The Protectors Series — Book One

Snowbound: The Protectors Series — Book Two

Pursued: The Protectors Series — Book Three

Three Short Stories Of Suspense: Deadly Thoughts, Secrets & The Plan

IMPOSTER

The Protectors Series – Book One

KAREN FENECH

IMPOSTER: The Protectors Series — Book One copyright © 2011 by Karen Fenech

Excerpt from SNOWBOUND: The Protectors Series — Book Two copyright © 2011 by Karen Fenech

Description for GONE copyright © 2009 by Karen Fenech

ALL RIGHTS RESERVED, including the right to reproduce this book or portions thereof in any form whatsoever. No part of this book may be reproduced, scanned, transmitted or distributed in any printed or electronic form, including digital, photocopying, recording or by any information storage and retrieval system without permission in writing from the author. Please do not participate in or encourage piracy of copyrighted materials in violation of the author's rights. Purchase only authorized editions.

This is a work of fiction. Names, characters, places and incidents are either the product of the author's imagination, or, if real, used fictitiously.

Edition: 2011
First Edition: February 2011

For Andrew

CHAPTER ONE

"Richard! Slow down!"

Heart pounding, Eve took her gaze from the road and cut a glance to the driver, Richard, her business partner.

Richard didn't respond. The CD player was blaring. Unlikely he could hear her above Van Halen's scream.

Richard had picked up his new Porsche just yesterday. He'd wanted to see what the car could do, he'd said with a smirk when they started on this road, and hit the gas. Now the road began to slope and the car gained additional speed. Eve's gaze went to the speedometer and her breath hitched. Ninety and climbing. Outside the passenger window, a view of trees and rock-face streaked by in a blur. Her mouth went dry.

Eve took her gaze from the road and cut a glance to Richard. His focus was trained on the rearview mirror.

It wasn't the first time in the last few minutes

she'd spotted him looking into the rearview. She looked around herself but couldn't see anything but the trail of dust the Porsche was kicking up in its wake. As she faced front again, again, Richard's focus lifted to the view behind them.

What was going on?

She reached out to lower the volume on the CD to ask him that question when the car swerved sharply to the right, throwing her toward the passenger door. The seatbelt held firm, preventing what could have been a nasty impact.

She returned her attention to Richard. Tension was now coming off him in waves. A fine sheen of sweat glistened on his brow. In his eyes, she saw terror.

Eve looked back. A dark sedan was now visible, moving fast and closing the distance between them.

"Richard, what's going on? Are we being followed?"

Richard didn't reply, but the Porsche shot forward with a sudden burst of speed. The sedan fell back but was picking up speed. It should have been no match for the Porsche but it continued to gain ground. Just what kind of engine was under the hood of that plain sedan? No ordinary sedan and Eve's nerves jumped.

Why were they being followed? Who would want to follow them?

The Porsche skidded. Richard steered into the skid. When the tires gained traction, he floored the gas pedal.

This was insane. If Richard and whoever was following them didn't slow down—

The road curved like a hair pin. Richard made a sound, but without breaking speed, drove into it. The rear fishtailed. Eve's breath caught. Richard cried out. Both his face and his grip on the steering wheel went white as he struggled to get the car under control. Eve's heart hammered. Each wild beat thundered in her ears.

"Richard!"

She turned to him. He was now slumped across the dashboard.

The speedometer read one-hundred-ten. The car raced out of control. Gravel pinged against the car's underside as the right front tire slid off the narrow strip of asphalt. The edge dropped off in a sheer cliff Eve couldn't see the bottom of.

Another instant and the car would go over.

Eve stared wide-eyed as the car continued to lose purchase. As the tires continued to slide away from the pavement. Was this how her life would end? In a car crash that would not right the wrong committed five years earlier when she had lived while the most precious thing in her world had died?

Tears filled her eyes. She thought back over the last five years to all of the times she'd wished she could go back to that moment and exchange her life for the one that was taken.

But she couldn't. She could not change the past. Not then and not now ...

The tires slid. The cliff loomed. The dark abyss drew closer.

Eve grabbed the steering wheel. Her hands were sweating. She latched on and jerked sharply to the right. The car veered away from the edge.

She shoved Richard toward the driver's door. He was a small, wiry man, but inert, his body was heavy. She grunted, heaved again, and he struck the driver's door hard. His blond head lolled against the window. He didn't protest her rough handling of him, not even a moan. Eve would have welcomed a moan. At the least he was unconscious. At the most ...

She fought off her fears for Richard. If she didn't stop the car, his condition would cease to matter—to both of them.

She grappled with her seat belt, releasing the catch, then slid onto the console and swung her leg over Richard's. She kicked his foot off the accelerator and stomped on the brake. The tires screeched as the car skidded, then went into a spin. The landscape of trees and rock face swirled by, then Eve didn't know if the car was again at the edge about to go over. She couldn't determine up or down. She'd lost her bearings.

She maintained her grip on the steering wheel and on the brake, the skin stretched taut over her knuckles, her teeth gritted as she fought to ride out the spin and regain control of the car.

The Porsche rocked to a stop. She was flung forward. Her instinctive grab of the dashboard twisted her wrist but saved her face. Laying her head on her arms, she closed her eyes and gave in to the weakness that had come over her now that the initial adrenaline rush was spent. Her ears were ringing. The car engine was now off and in the silence she could hear herself breathing. Shallow, panting gasps for air that hurt to inhale and exhale. Other than those complaints, she felt fine. Alive.

Richard ...

She turned to him and shook his shoulder. He didn't respond. She pressed her fingertips to his neck. Her hands were shaking so badly she wasn't sure she'd detect any other movement, but she felt a thready pulse.

She'd bought a bottle of water at the last gas station they'd stopped at. It was in the cup holder. She uncapped it and upended it onto Richard's face. Water flowed down his shaved cheeks.

Eve tapped the back of her hand against his skin. "Richard."

He didn't respond. She struck him harder. His cheek reddened. She'd hit him hard enough to mark him, but apparently not enough to rouse him.

"Hang on, Richard," she murmured.

She turned the key, but the engine didn't start. Her purse ... where was her purse? She spotted the little envelope bag on the floorboard. She fumbled with the snap and yanked out her cell phone. She had to get help.

Where were they? She glanced around the deserted stretch of road. A meadow lay beyond the two lanes of asphalt. Trees and scraggly bushes grew on the grass, amid patches of white and yellow wildflowers. She and Richard had left Manhattan bound for Rowland, a county in Pennsylvania, about an hour ago. They were chemists and they were on their way to a chemist's conference in Pittsburgh. Richard had kept to back roads like this one to avoid traffic.

Other than the sedan that was no longer in sight, she couldn't remember the last time they came across another car. None were in sight now. The sun was lowering behind a cluster of oaks. Nightfall was imminent. If this road was rarely traveled in daylight, what was the likelihood of another car coming along at night? With Richard in his present condition, they could not pass the night here. She pushed dark hair back from her face and flipped open the phone.

An instant later she found there was no signal. She hoped that was because she was inside the car. As she was about to go outside and try the phone again, the sedan that had been following them skidded to a halt behind the Porsche.

Both the driver and passenger doors were flung open. Two men charged out. One man was dark-haired, the other blond. Both wore suits and ties.

Eve wanted to be away from there. She knew nothing about the occupants of that car other than that Richard had been terrified of them. But where to go? She was in the middle of nowhere. The car disabled. Her phone useless. She had no weapon to defend herself and Richard. She'd turned in her service weapon years ago along with her resignation from the LAPD.

To buy a moment to think, she reached out to engage the automatic door locks. Ineffective if these men were armed, but if not, the locked doors would keep them at bay.

Before she could hit the locks, both her door and Richard's door were thrown open. The dark haired man bent over Richard. The blond man reached for her.

Eve drew back. "I don't know who you are or what you want, but Richard needs help. He needs a doctor."

The dark-haired man glanced at Eve. His eyes, dark brown and deep-set, narrowed to slits. He pressed his lips together, tight enough that a line formed on either side of his mouth. There was no mistaking his anger, though she could not account for it.

The blond man's soft, doughy features were grim. Eve's heart pounded. She looked from one man to the other. "Why are you just standing around?" She was afraid she knew, but blurted out anyway. "We need to get Richard to a doctor. Now."

"Richard is dead," the dark-haired man said bluntly.

As he stepped back from the open doorway, back from Richard, she glimpsed her business partner, slumped against the black leather seat. His eyes were glazed. There was no mistaking the vacant look in them now and the gray cast to his skin that indicated recent death.

Eve continued to stare at him. She shook her head, not wanting to believe what she was seeing.

At any moment she expected him to bounce up and burst into movement. But he did not.

Richard ...

Tears burned her eyes. She pressed her fingers to them. Her hands trembled. She clenched them briefly in an effort to steady them. The need to know how Richard died weighed on her, along with a terrible sadness. She and Richard had been partners for four years and though that relationship had its ups and downs—was presently down—she felt a loss at his passing. Now was not the time for questions, though, or to mourn. She had to keep it together and see him home.

"Let's get him into our car," the dark-haired man said.

The men hooked Richard beneath the arms and legs, and removed him from his vehicle. They hauled him across the asphalt to their own car and stuffed him into the trunk. The act galvanized Eve. Richard was dead. Why had they moved him?

Eve left the Porsche and stumbled out onto the asphalt. She was still holding her phone and dropped it onto the pavement as she ran to the sedan.

She reached it and seized the lid just as the dark-haired man was about to slam it. "You can't move Richard's body. Drive back to the nearest city and send the police." What was the name of the last place they drove through? She shook her head in frustration. She couldn't recall it. She eyed the two men. "There's a city about a forty minute drive east of here. Since you were on this road, you would have passed it as well. There's bound to be a police station there."

The man slammed the trunk and turned to his companion. "You'd better get going. I'll be in touch."

"Will do."

The men acted as if she hadn't spoken. Eve reached out and seized the dark-haired man's forearm. Beneath the conservative gray suit was hard muscle. Instead of digging into skin, her nails bent. She bit down hard on her back teeth "Did you hear what I said?"

He met her gaze. "Every word. I'm afraid, however, that we *will* be removing the body."

She could see the promise in his eyes, and her anger spiked another notch. "Listen to me— "

"Dr. Collins—"

"You know me?" She searched her memory, but could not recall ever meeting him. He obviously knew her, and though he had yet to harm her, that fact unsettled her, reminded her that this man and his companion had been following Richard.

Who were these men? Eve's stomach went as tight as a fist. Her body went cold with apprehension but she knew better than to show it. She crossed her arms and narrowed her gaze on the dark-haired man who appeared to be leading the other man. "I asked you a question."

"We've never met. I'm John Burke." Burke indicated the man beside him. "This is Michael Lanski. We work for a division of the Central Intelligence Agency." Burke withdrew a small folder from inside his suit jacket and opened it for her inspection. It was his picture ID. He replaced it, then repeated to Lanski, "Get going."

Lanski got behind the wheel of the sedan, and Eve's heart thumped. "Where is he going?" she asked Burke. "Why were you following Richard? What does the CIA want with Richard's body?"

"We'll talk on the drive to Rowland," Burke said. "Let's go, Dr. Collins."

Eve narrowed her eyes on Burke. "You know

where Richard and I were going?"

Burke gave her a level look. "Oh, yeah. We know a lot of things about you and Richard."

Eve arched her eyebrows at the cryptic statement. "What is that supposed to mean?"

Before Burke could respond—if he'd intended to—Eve's attention was drawn by the sedan. Lanski spun the car in a U-turn then, tires squealing, sped down the road. Dust swirled in the air where the car had been an instant earlier, and Richard was gone.

Again, Eve felt tears burn. She forced them back and confronted Burke. "I asked you what the CIA wants with Richard's body."

"And I told you we would talk on the way to Rowland," Burke said.

The sun had lowered and dusk had descended. In the interval between day and night, there was a stillness, a quiet time. In the silence, Eve became aware of the hum of the Porsche's engine. She'd thought the car was disabled by the accident, but Burke or Lanski had started it. Obviously, Burke intended that they leave there in Richard's vehicle.

Eve crossed her arms. "I'm not going anywhere with you, Mr. Burke."

He braced his hands low on his hips. "Are you thinking to wait out here, hoping another car will come along?"

"Oh, no. I am leaving. You're not. I'm taking the car. You should have gone with Lanski." Eve's cheeks warmed. "This isn't over. If you won't tell me what I want to know, I'll get my answers from your office. I will get Richard's body released. I will find out why the CIA even knows my name."

Eve moved past him toward the car.

"You aren't going anywhere without me."

She glanced back at Burke. He hadn't moved, but his eyes had hardened and she knew he meant what he said. He outweighed her by at least seventy pounds and topped her by a good eight inches. Did he intend to use physical force to detain her? On the job, she'd taken down men of his size before. Still, he would need a reason to insist that she accompany him. He was an officer of the law, after all, not a thug.

She raised an eyebrow. "If you want to stop me, you're going to have to place me under arrest."

Burke reached into a back pocket and held up a pair of handcuffs.

Eve's lips tensed briefly. "You have to be out of your mind, Burke. I'm a chemist not a criminal."

"You set the terms, Doctor. We are going to talk. If I have to arrest you to do that, I will."

"This is ridiculous. You can't arrest me without cause."

"Oh, I have cause." He leaned in close to her, and his voice lowered to a near whisper. "You've been named in a terrorist plot, Doctor. The charge for committing an offence against your country is treason."

CHAPTER TWO

"Treason? You really are out of your mind, Burke," Eve said.

In the scant day light that remained, she eyed Burke's tensed features. It was still just the two of them on this back road. The bushes and trees that dotted the flat landscape were dark smudges against the ever-darkening sky, adding to the feeling of isolation.

She pitched her voice to be heard above the idling engine of Richard's car and the call of a Loon. "I don't have time for your wild tale. I need to notify Richard's family about his death."

"You won't be notifying anyone yet," Burke said.

The day had cooled with the onset of evening. The slight breeze now felt too cold. Goose bumps sprang on her bare arms. She rubbed her skin to warm it.

"What?" she said. "Of course, I'm going to let Richard's parents know he's dead."

"I can't let you do that."

Though spoken softly, there was an edge to the statement that sounded like a command and Eve straightened her shoulders. "You have custody of Richard's body for the moment, but I can and will call the Pattersons about their son."

Burke shook his head slowly. "At this point, revealing that Richard is dead will compromise our national security."

Eve let Burke hear how ridiculous she found that statement in her sharp tone. "Richard was no threat to the security of our country."

Burke replaced the handcuffs he held in a back pocket and met her glare. "We've learned that Richard Patterson, and an accomplice we've determined is you, created and are marketing a formula for a deadly chemical agent."

"You think we're terrorists?" Eve pressed her lips together briefly. "Hear me: Richard and I develop perfumes and cosmetics."

She and Richard started their business four years earlier. Richard, whom she'd met through mutual friends, had approached her to become his partner. Though she hadn't acknowledged it then, his offer was a life-line to her. Her career with the LAPD had ended shortly before under a cloud of scandal. Her marriage fell apart and her worst fear was realized: Emily died. Her bright and beautiful little girl was lost to her forever.

Recalling that day tore Eve's heart. She fought back the pain of Emily's death and forced herself to focus on Burke.

"Our business has earned a solid reputation in the industry that I take great pride in," Eve said.

"Sorry to disappoint you, Burke, but the most deadly formula we've created is a kick-ass anti-wrinkle cream."

Burke crossed his arms. "We know that you and Richard are planning to meet a buyer for your formula tomorrow."

"Tomorrow Richard and I were scheduled to attend a series of lectures at a chemist's conference in Pittsburgh which you know about. We had no appointments."

Burke went on as if she hadn't spoken. "Your meeting is set for tomorrow evening at the cottage Richard Patterson rented for your three night stay in Rowland."

The cottage. Eve rolled her eyes. A get-back-to-nature place that was a ninety minute drive from the hotel where the conference was being held had not been her ideal accommodation for a business trip. She would never have expected city-lover Richard to make that choice. He was no outdoors man and his claim of wanting to get away from the city and enjoy some quiet time in a country setting had struck her as out of character. Then again, little about Richard's behavior in recent months had been what she was used to from him.

The perpetually surly Richard had been in an unusually happy frame of mind that he didn't elaborate on when she commented on it. She'd mentioned it to him again as she'd buckled her seat belt earlier that day. He'd turned to her and smiled, showing deep dimples and the beautiful results of a small fortune in orthodontics, then turned up Van Halen and began to move in time with the music. Every part of his body that she could see was in some kind of motion. He was as close to dancing as a person could get in a seated position.

She didn't begrudge him his good mood, but she resented that since it started, his work had plummeted. He was a brilliant chemist but he seemed to have lost all interest in their business. Clients were complaining and the company lost two long- standing contracts with cosmetics manufacturers. They would have lost a third if, at the eleventh hour, she hadn't completed and submitted a formula for a new perfume he'd abandoned.

Eve's lips tensed briefly as she recalled that incident and how he shrugged it off as unimportant. After that, she was half-expecting him to tell her he wanted to end their partnership. She would have been very sorry they came to that after all they went through to establish themselves, but would have agreed it was for the best. She was considering making the suggestion herself when he announced he wanted to go with her to the conference. She attended every year but he never went, proclaiming it a dead bore.

When he mentioned going along, she thought he may be looking to regain his enthusiasm for their work. If so, she felt he deserved that chance. She put the thought of ending their partnership on hold.

None of that mattered now, though.

An image of Richard as she'd last seen him - in the trunk of the sedan - flashed in her mind. She blinked to clear it then allowed a moment to pass while she regained her composure before returning her attention to Burke. "Like I said, our business is cosmetics. You have the wrong people, Burke."

"We have Patterson nailed and as for you, Patterson himself named you as his accomplice."

"That's impossible."

Burke's eyes narrowed. Fine lines appeared in the skin around them. "Patterson made it known to his buyer that he was working with you."

"This makes no sense."

Burke ignored her comment and went on. "I searched Patterson's body before Lanski and I moved it. I found some papers in his jacket pocket." He reached into the breast pocket of his own suit. The crisp white shirt beneath was revealed and seemed to glow in the twilight. He withdrew two folded pages and held them out to her. "Interesting reading."

Eve snatched the papers from him and unfolded them. The messy letters and numbers that slanted sharply to the right were unmistakably Richard's scribble. She squinted to make out his handwriting in the lengthening shadows. She expected to find a formula for one of the perfumes or face creams Richard had been working on. It was his habit to record his notes on paper rather than onto his laptop and risk losing his work in a computer crash. What she read, however, was no formula for scent. The ingredients listed formed a deadly chemical compound with an organophosphate anticholinesterase base like the lethal nerve agent

Sarin. Richard had taken the process to another level, creating an agent that required less of the chemical to kill and would do so faster. Eve's mouth went dry.

Her hand that held the formula dropped to her side. She felt as if she'd been punched in the stomach. She lowered her gaze to Richard's formula. The papers fluttered in the slight breeze, defying her to deny them.

Which, of course, she could not.

How could Richard do this? The anger at Burke drained out of her, replaced by horror. "If this formula were used, so many people could die," she mumbled. A coldness crept over her that had nothing to do with the chill in the air and she shivered.

"Am I supposed to be impressed by your performance?"

Eve's cheeks warmed at Burke's unwarranted attack on her character. "I don't give a damn about impressing you. I had no clue what Richard was working on." She tightened her fingers into a fist, angry with herself over that. Irrational anger. It wasn't her job to keep tabs on Richard.

"Save it for the courtroom," Burke said.

Eve took a step toward Burke. "You can't mean you intend to pursue this?" Her voice rose. "Richard is dead and I'm telling you I don't know anything other than what you've told me."

"And I told you that Richard claimed you were partners in this plot. We've been watching you both for months. We intended to apprehend the two of you and your buyer at tomorrow's meeting but Patterson's death necessitated that you and I talk before that meeting takes place."

"Richard is dead. You sound as if the meeting is still on."

"Oh, it's on. I'm going to take Patterson's place."

"You?" Eve raised her brows. "You intend to impersonate Richard? Don't you think whoever was planning to meet Richard will notice you're not him?"

The physical differences were impossible to disguise. Dye could change Burke's dark hair to Richard's blond, but there was no way to mistake Burke's greater height and solid athletic build for Richard's slight frame.

"We know that Richard and the buyer have never met," Burke said. "That works out well for us, under the circumstances, and makes it possible for me to take his place. I want you to accompany me. I want you to introduce me as Richard at the conference to lend credibility to the deception. The buyer, as you know, is expecting to meet with you both."

Eve shook her head. "There will be someone at the conference who'll know you're not Richard—his accomplice. I am not that person."

Burke ignored her comment. "I can't force you to attend the conference with me, of course, but if you refuse, I will have you transported to Washington immediately for questioning. The choice is yours."

"Sending me to Washington would be a waste of time. I. Don't. Know. Anything." Eve enunciated each word.

Burke let her see his disbelief and derision in

his eyes. "What'll it be Doctor—the conference or Washington?"

Eve couldn't believe this was happening. That Richard was dead. That he'd created a deadly chemical weapon for terrorists. That she was believed to be working for terrorists as well. Cold sweat broke out on her spine. Fear sweat. She didn't want to go to the conference and put on this charade, but she didn't want to go to Washington either to be questioned when she had no answers to give in her own defense.

She needed a moment to think without Burke's razor sharp gaze on her and gave him her back, turning away from his scrutiny.

She stared into the darkness as she considered her options. If she went to Washington— game over. Some option. She closed her eyes and exhaled a shaky, fearful breath at that finality.

The conference then? But if she accompanied Burke to the conference, would she only be delaying the inevitable? The inevitable ... Eve pushed the frightening thought away and forced herself to move on.

Burke had said that Richard and his accomplice were going to meet their buyer. Since the accomplice wouldn't know Richard was dead, that person would have no reason to deviate from the plan to attend the meeting. When he did show himself, she would be exonerated.

Eve rubbed her temples. Burke's plan had merit. He had inadvertently come up with a plan that would prove her innocence. He would certainly apprehend the accomplice without her, but being with him ensured that she was in the loop. She'd been a good cop once—her dishonorable departure from the force didn't change that truth. And just now, she welcomed the opportunity to take this active role.

Eve took a deep breath of the crisp night air. The breeze shifted and she inhaled the sweet scent of lilacs from a bush that was now cloaked by the night. "Okay, Burke. I'll go along with your plan."

"What was your relationship with Patterson?"

"What?"

"If I'm going to impersonate him, I need to know how to act with you. There'll be people at the conference you've seen year after year. You've probably spoken of personal matters. I don't want anything to raise any red flags."

"Your surveillance didn't give you any juicy details?"

She resented the impertinent question that invaded her privacy, but he had a point. Though she only saw these chemists once a year, they had exchanged jokes about their love lives—and lack-there-of. She had fielded questions on a number of occasions about the nature of her "business" with her partner.

Reminding herself that she needed Burke to be credible as Richard so the accomplice, if he were observing them, would go through with the meeting, she decided to answer his question. It was easy enough to do that. She and Richard were never romantically involved. He'd attempted to initiate an affair early in their partnership. Casual sex wasn't her style and with Richard that's all there would be. He was self-absorbed and she was not attracted to his pretty boy looks. She preferred rugged handsomeness, the kind that Burke possessed. She frowned. She didn't care for the thought and dismissed it.

"Richard and I had a business relationship," Eve said. "Nothing more."

Burke nodded. "Let's get going."

"Before we leave here, I need to take an insulin injection. I'm diabetic."

She didn't think her condition would come as a surprise to him. Her medical history would have been included in his investigation of her.

Without waiting for his response, she went to the car. Burke followed her.

Her cell phone lay on the pavement. He picked it up. "Yours?"

At her nod, he handed it to her. She returned it to her purse and retrieved the two pen injectors containing her insulin and an alcohol wipe. She was on two different types of insulin, a regular and a rapid-acting. She read the labels, selected the injector with the regular insulin for night time. Leaning against the passenger side, she left the car door open to provide light and after a swipe of alcohol across her upper arm, administered the injection. Burke stood by in silence. After, she added the needle to a plastic container where she'd discarded two others she'd used earlier in the day. She'd dispose of them properly when she reached the cottage.

"You take three injections daily?"

Burke knew the number, confirming her earlier assumption that he knew of her condition.

She swatted a mosquito that was drawn to the

light. “Yes. This is the last.”

He nodded. “Do you need a moment before we can leave?”

Eve raised one eyebrow. “Your concern is touching, but I’m good to go.”

“Make no mistake, Doctor, my only concern is that you remain well for questioning.”

Eve straightened her spine. “Of course. Can’t have your suspect die on you before you deliver me to Washington.” Eve turned away from him and got into the car. “Get a move on, Burke. We still have a long drive to the cottage.”

Burke glanced at his watch. “We won’t be going directly to the cottage. We have to make a stop first.”

CHAPTER THREE

The stop turned out to be a diner on a country road.

"This is the stop?" Eve made no effort to hide her impatience.

"I could go for something to eat," Burke said, turning the car into a gravel parking lot. "How about you?"

The dashboard clock in the car read eight-eleven p.m. She'd been late finishing work at the lab, in anticipation of her three day absence, and missed lunch. The idea of food wasn't unappealing, but the notion of sitting down to a meal with Burke, the normalcy of it, struck her as incongruous given their circumstances. Still, she needed to eat. *Had to* was more like it, whether she was hungry or not because of her diabetic condition. After three years of living with the disease, she'd learned the routine and respected the necessity of adhering to it. But it left her feeling vulnerable. She didn't care for the feeling.

Burke parked beside the only other vehicle on the lot, a pickup in need of a wash, and turned off the car engine. The diner was back lit by the lowering sun, lending a red glow to the peeling whitewashed structure.

Burke took his black wallet out of the inside pocket of his jacket. The shoulder holster beneath and the gun it held were revealed for an instant. He opened the wallet, and again Eve glimpsed his picture ID as he extracted a pair of twenties. He slid the wallet beneath the driver's seat.

It was an odd thing to do and Eve was sure her facial expression reflected that thought, but she said nothing. If he chose to be careless with his Agency ID, then that was his concern.

"Ready?" Burke asked.

Before she could answer, he was standing on the gravel and swinging the car door to a close.

The atmosphere inside the diner was cozy. Small round tables lined two walls. Garth Brooks crooned a soft country tune from a radio atop the long counter that glistened from the wipe-down it was getting from a waitress.

They took seats by the window. She expected Burke to choose a location that backed against a wall. He didn't. Too many spy novels, she supposed, had fostered that idea. Seated across from him, she acknowledged that though he lacked the polished looks of the actors who'd portrayed the James Bond character in the movies, Burke would have done that character justice on the Hollywood screen just the same. His suit covered what appeared to be a hard, athletic body. The light shadow of beard that now darkened his cheeks and jaw added to his sexy appeal.

Not that how he looked mattered to her.

The waitress left the counter and ambled up to their table. Eve was glad of the distraction.

"We're about ready to close," the woman said. Deep grooves dug into the sides of her mouth and brow as she spoke. "Grill's been cleaned." She tilted her head and the purple stones in her earrings twinkled in the light. "The best I can offer you at this point is a cup of coffee and a sandwich."

"That'll be fine," Burke said.

The waitress ticked off the choices on her fingers. "Ham and Swiss or Tuna Salad."

"Tuna," Eve said.

"The same. And the coffee you mentioned would be great. Black, for me. Eve?"

"Black for me, too—Bu—John."

Clearly she wasn't any good at this cloak and dagger stuff, but if the waitress noticed that Eve had almost called her companion by the wrong name, she didn't react.

"I'll be right back with your coffees," the waitress said.

Eve stretched out her arms on the wooden tabletop and linked her fingers in a tight grip. By this time tomorrow night, she should be on her way back home. That Richard had used his skill to harm anyone angered her. She could not comprehend how he would have done this. As much as she was angry at Burke for refusing to listen when she told him she was innocent, she was glad that he'd learned what Richard was planning before he could sell the formula.

She focused on Burke. "How did you find out what Richard was involved in?"

Burke raised a dark eyebrow in a mocking gesture. Eve leaned as far forward as the edge of the tabletop allowed. "Can your sarcasm for a minute and answer my question."

Burke leveled his gaze on her. "He let it be known that he could be hired to develop chemical weapons. He answered a personal ad on a website we've been monitoring for terrorist activity. That ad was a cover for a request for a chemical weapon."

"That's how these people contact each other?"

"That's one way."

Clearly Burke had no intention of elaborating. She would not have credited Richard with knowing how to initiate such contact. Again, she was struck by the fact that she'd been clueless to what was going on right under her nose.

The waitress arrived with their coffees. Eve sat back as the steaming cup was set in front of her. When they were alone again, she asked, "Do you know why Richard got involved with these people?" A terrible thought occurred to her. "Richard wasn't married. His parents are his only family." Eve's stomach tightened at the thought they might have been threatened. "Could it have been about more than money?"

"A great deal of money, Doctor," Burke said. "If you're thinking he was pressured or threatened to cooperate, he wasn't."

The waitress returned and placed their dinner orders in front of them. She left the check by the plates in a not-so-subtle hint that their time was limited.

Burke picked up his sandwich and dug in. Eve took a couple of bites but found she wasn't as hungry as she had been a few moments ago. The gravity of her situation struck her again. She picked up her coffee and held it between both hands as she took a long sip. The air conditioner in the diner kicked on making a loud hum and a middle aged man wearing a white T-shirt molded to his lean body started a floor polisher. The combined sounds made conversation impossible, which Eve was glad of. She had nothing to say to Burke at the moment and nothing she wished to hear from him.

Burke pointed to her plate and raised an eyebrow. "Problem with your sandwich?"

Eve shook her head. "It's fine."

Burke didn't press. The next few moments were passed in silence as he finished eating.

"You done?" he asked.

Eve nodded. Burke placed one of the twenties he'd taken from his wallet on the table to take care of the check. Eve got to her feet and preceded him out of the diner.

A third vehicle was parked in the lot when Eve and Burke reached it. An early model mini van. The windows were covered by curtains patterned with grinning cows.

An elderly couple strolled around the Porsche. The man was tall with a full head of silver hair. He smiled as he reached out and patted the rooftop.

"Good evening to you," the man said. His accent was unmistakably southern. "My wife and

I were admiring your very fine ve-hic-le."

That's right." The woman nodded. She wore a straw hat with a ribbon bow tipped back on her head. "We had an early model way back when, didn't we Harry?"

"My, yes. It has been some time." He released a deep breath and without taking his eyes from the car asked, "Mind if we take a look inside?"

"Be my guest," Burke said.

Eve glanced at her watch. They really had to be on their way.

"This sure does take me back," Harry said from behind the wheel. He sighed long in appreciation and caressed the leather wrapped steering wheel as if it were a lover. His wife slid into the passenger side and the couple sat together in a companionable silence.

The man reached out and clasped his wife's hand then brought it to his lips. Her light blue eyes grew warm on her husband's face.

Despite her impatience to be on her way, Eve couldn't help but be touched by them, touched and a little wistful. Once, she too, had expected to share a lifetime with her own husband.

"Maybe we ought to just get ourselves one of these again? How about that Mary?" Harry winked at his wife.

She laughed.

With a loud and obviously reluctant sigh, Harry stepped out of the car. He extended his hand to Burke. "Thank you, kindly. Appreciate you letting us reminisce."

"My pleasure," Burke said.

Harry turned to Eve and shook her hand as

well.

"Drive safe," Mary added.

Eve watched them enter the diner. "That was a nice thing you just did, Burke."

"I can be nice."

"I'll reserve judgment on that," she said.

Without replying, Burke got behind the wheel. They buckled up and left the parking lot. Night had fallen and the moon roof showed the sky lit with stars. Moonlight illuminated the inside of the car. Burke popped the Van Halen CD out of the player, and selected a radio station that played fifties and sixties rock. At the moment, Rick Nelson was singing about "Mary Lou".

Eve rested her head back against the seat. Lulled by the soft purr of the engine and the music, she felt she could fall asleep. She couldn't believe that, given what was going on in her life now, and given that she was in the company of a man she'd known for only a few hours.

Burke slid his wallet out from under the driver's seat. Not his wallet, Eve realized, this one was brown.

She sat upright. "That's not the wallet you stashed under the seat before we went into the diner."

Burke met her gaze. "No." He flipped open the wallet revealing a driver's license, passport, social security card, and an assortment of credit cards. The name on each piece of identification was Richard Patterson, but the photos verifying the ID were all of Burke.

"Then how did you—" Her eyes narrowed as she figured it out. "The elderly couple."

Eve tapped the wallet. "This was why you wanted to stop here. Those people delivered new ID for you. They work for you, Burke."

"Not Burke. Richard. From here on, I'm Richard Patterson."

* * *

They arrived at the cottage in Rowland in the early hours of the morning. For the most part, the streets they'd driven by were all dark, Eve noticed. Apparently, the residents of Rowland were not people who stayed up into the wee hours of the morning.

As described, the cottage was on an isolated stretch of land. It looked to be built about forty years back when land could be had in abundance for a reasonable price, as opposed to the near postage-sized lots available now and sold at a premium.

Burke parked in front of the small dwelling and they left the car. He unlocked the door to the cottage. Apparently when he and Lanski searched Richard's body earlier, they came up with more than the notes on the formula, Eve observed. They'd also found the keys Richard had received from the agent he'd rented the cottage from.

Burke switched on the overhead lights and Eve followed him into one large room. Curtains on the windows were open, letting in the moonlight. The place was inviting with a large couch filled with thick-stuffed cushions. A brick fireplace took up a large portion of one wall. A framed photograph of a bird poised for flight was centered above the fireplace. The photo was slightly askew.

From where she stood at the door, Eve could also see the kitchen. The room was painted a cornflower blue with medium oak accents that gave a warm and homey atmosphere. She took a step, intent on checking out the two bedrooms, but Burke placed his hand on her arm.

"Give me a minute," he said.

Without waiting for her reply, Burke strode into the nearest room. She supposed his training had him looking under table cloths and peeking around corners. When she'd been on the police force, she'd maintained an awareness of her surroundings, but several years out of that life had taken the suspicion off and she'd gotten out of the habit.

Still, in their case, she wasn't sure it was just carefully honed habit that had Burke checking their surroundings.

"Well?" she asked when he was back in the living room area with her.

"All clear." He slid the gun he'd drawn back in his shoulder holster.

"Any reason to think it might not have been?"

Burke remained silent for an instant, then met her gaze. "Richard Patterson died abruptly. We won't know what caused his death until the autopsy results are in."

"You think Richard may have been murdered?"

"I don't think it. I'm just being cautious. I can't see anyone killing him and not taking the formula. Like I said, I'm just being cautious."

Burke was right. It made no sense for the accomplice or buyer to kill Richard and not take the formula. Besides, Burke said that Richard had never met the people he'd entered into this alliance with.

"I'll get our bags," Burke said.

Eve followed him to the car. It was late. She didn't plan on unpacking now.

All she wanted was the garment bag that held the suit she planned to wear in the morning for the conference and her makeup case and hair dryer.

When Burke would have grabbed her suitcase as well as his own, she shook her head. "I just want what I'll need for the morning." She followed up her words by swinging out the garment bag and grabbing the makeup case and hair dryer, then returning to the cabin.

She chose the first room off the short hall and shut the door behind herself.

* * *

Burke watched Eve walk away from him. Against his will, his gaze lingered. He took in her straight back, the sweep of her dark hair across her shoulders, the narrow curve of her waistline. With a scowl, he looked away from her.

He was angry, his body tense with it. This investigation that should have clicked into place had blown apart. Richard Patterson was dead and now, here Burke was, forced to take Patterson's place. What should have been a cut and dried apprehension had become complicated. And, instead of overseeing the investigation, where he needed to be, he'd had to hand over that responsibility to his second in command Lanski while he was now stuck in the middle of nowhere impersonating Patterson and guarding his accomplice.

Burke pulled out his cell phone and called Lanski.

"Hey, boss," Lanski said an instant later. "Are you calling from the road?"

Burke's cell phone was secure so his location could not be determined. "No. We've arrived."

"You and the lady doc all settled in?"

That comment brought on another scowl. Burke ignored the question and asked his own. "Are we set for tomorrow night?"

"All set, sir," Lanski said, all humor gone. "We'll have the cottage covered with land, sea and air surveillance. Just like you ordered. The buyer won't get away from us."

Burke expected nothing less. "Dr. Collins still has her cell phone in her possession."

"You let her keep it?"

"Yeah. I want you to monitor her cell phone calls. Incoming and outgoing. I want to know who she calls and who calls her."

Lanski paused briefly then said, "You want to know if she tips anyone off about Patterson?"

"Yeah."

"Good thinking. She might not be expecting that we'll be listening, and have her guard down. I'm on it. Anything else?"

"That's it for now."

"See you tomorrow night."

"Tomorrow," Burke repeated.

This would all be over then. He couldn't wait.

CHAPTER FOUR

They were on the road at seven-thirty the next morning. If this had been another day, Eve would have welcomed an additional couple of hours of sleep. She wasn't a morning person to begin with and topping that with the sleepless night spent worrying over her situation had left her edgy. But, this was the day the true accomplice would reveal himself and exonerate her. She couldn't get the day started early enough.

They stopped for breakfast at a restaurant in Rowland then resumed the drive to the conference. Burke didn't ask for directions to the hotel where the conference was being held. It was clear that he knew exactly where he was headed. When they arrived, he pulled into the valet parking. The act was so typically Richard that Eve glanced over at the man behind the wheel. The hotel allowed for patrons to park their own vehicles, but Eve had never known Richard to do that when someone else was available to park his car for him. She wondered if Burke was acting as Burke or if he was mimicking Richard's behavior. He was falling into impersonating Richard well.

Her door was opened by the hotel attendant who offered his hand to help her out. Eve placed her hand in his and stepped onto the asphalt. The day was overcast, but despite the clouds covering the sun, the air outside was warm and sticky.

Burke—ah, Richard—she had to remember to call him Richard—joined her and they made their way through the double glass doors that accessed the hotel lobby.

The conference coordinators reserved the same rooms for the event each year. For the first time since she'd embarked on the trip with Richard, Eve knew where she was heading.

She spotted Matt Deligne making his way toward her. Deligne was a big, bold Texan, topping six feet by several inches. His shaggy hair, beneath a white Stetson, was sun-streaked, attesting to the time he spent outdoors on the cattle ranch he lived on.

"Why hi y'all," he said, when he reached her. He swept her into a bear hug that squeezed a cough from her.

After Eve extracted herself from Deligne's hold, she said, "Richard, this is Matt Deligne. Matt, my business partner, Richard Patterson."

"Matt," Burke said.

Burke and Deligne shook hands.

"Never did see you out this way, Rick," Deligne said. "Have to say, I was starting to believe Eve had made you all up as an excuse to deny going out with me."

"As you can see, Matt, Richard is very real." Eve had to force the smile that she needed to go along with that statement about Richard.

"Well, I've never been one to back away from competition," Matt said.

She added softly, not wishing to cause Matt hurt. "Richard isn't the reason you and I will go on being just friends."

Beside her, Burke tensed. Maybe in anticipation of Matt's reaction, but Eve had never known Matt to be anything but good-natured.

Matt laughed now, loud enough that patrons at the other end of the long hall way glanced in their direction. "I think the lady just hit me dead-on with a solid right hook. I'm bleeding all over this fancy carpeting, darlin'."

She'd been less than tactful and her words hadn't come out as she'd intended. She was sorry for that. The last thing she wanted was to cause her friend hurt. "Sorry, Matt. It isn't you, it's me." God, she was making things worse with the trite line.

Matt laughed. "Easy. You can quit dancing now. My heart's bruised but still beating." He winked at her. "And here comes Allie. I know you'll be glad to see him."

"Allie" was Alasdair McHampton, a Scotsman who emigrated to the United States from Edinburgh in the nineteen fifties. He'd retired from researching pharmaceuticals years back, but missed being able to discuss his passion for chemistry and sought out the conference and like-minded individuals each year to indulge in conversation he was no longer able to have elsewhere.

Allie's thinning, sandy blond hair stood up in places. His shirt was slightly creased and his signature polka dot bow tie was askew. As usual, Allie looked rumpled. Eve found Allie's rumpled state endearing. Of their little group, Allie was the one she was most fond of, and the one person she kept in touch with apart from the conference. She'd invited him out to visit her in New York in the past, but the elderly gentleman had regretfully refused. He was terrified of flying and prone to car sickness. If he didn't live in the vicinity of this hotel, it was doubtful that he would attend the conference.

When Allie joined them, Eve reached out and embraced him.

"You have brightened this room with your presence my dear," Allie said.

Eve laughed. "It's good to see you, Allie."

She straightened the bow tie for him, as she usually did several times during the course of the conference, then introduced Burke as Richard. She did so reluctantly. She hated perpetuating the deception on Allie.

"So this is your mystery man." Allie clasped Burke's hand in a firm shake.

Eve grinned at Allie's description. Though he had never married himself, he was quite the romantic. Allie was something of a matchmaker and after learning that she was no longer married kept a watchful eye for prospective candidates for her affection.

Allie quickly engaged Burke in conversation. As usual, Allie's topic of choice was chemistry and

Eve's stomach tightened. Burke hadn't been expecting to have to step in and impersonate a chemist. Did he even know anything about chemistry? If so, did he know enough to be able to fool a professional?

Part of her wanted the smug Burke to fall on his face and she imagined herself apologizing to Allie for the deception when Burke slipped up. The more practical part of her, though, knew in order for the suspicion against her to go away, for Burke himself to go away, Burke's impersonation had to work. She was thinking of how to rescue him from the conversation when it soon became apparent that Burke didn't need a rescue. He was holding up his end with Allie just fine.

"Dr. Abernathy is about to begin his talk very shortly," Allie said with a broad smile. "I don't want to miss that. Shall we proceed?"

Eve fell into step beside Allie, leaving Burke, and Matt Deligne to follow. Inside the conference room, Eve set her purse on the floor and took a seat beside Allie. Burke sat on Eve's other side. Though Eve usually enjoyed the seminars scheduled at this conference, and partook of as many of them as she could fit into the tight three days, she couldn't have been less interested now. Keynote speaker Dr. Gerald Abernathy was introduced, made his way to the podium, and began to speak. Eve glanced at her watch. She'd never known time to move so slowly. She wanted it to be midnight and to be back at the cottage with the meeting with the buyer underway.

Abernathy droned on. By the avid expressions on the faces of the people around her, his audience was enthralled. Allie, in particular, had slid forward and now sat on the end of his seat. Eve shifted position in the plush chair. She moved several times more on the taupe cushion then Burke's arm snaked around her shoulders, stilling her.

He leaned toward her and whispered in her ear. "You're wearing a hole in that chair."

Of course, he was calm. This was a job to him. Business as usual. To her it was her life. Before she could give Burke that reply, Abernathy announced that he would be taking a brief intermission. Eve broke Burke's grip on her shoulders and shot to her feet.

"Fascinating. Positively fascinating," Allie said. He rose slowly to his feet. "I think I'll help myself to some refreshment."

A table took up a portion of one wall and wait staff bustled about setting covered dishes and trays on the white covering.

Allie glanced from Eve to Burke and then to Matt who now formed a semi-circle around him. "Anyone care to join me?"

Matt clapped Allie on the shoulder. "I'm with you."

Allie turned to Eve. "How about you my dear?"

"Sounds good."

Allie offered his arm.

A cell phone rang. Burke retrieved the ringing phone from his pocket. Richard's phone, Eve realized. His name was stamped on the cover. The formula. The keys to the cottage. The cell phone. Burke had been thorough when he'd searched Richard's body.

Burke glanced at the telephone briefly, checking the caller ID. Eve leaned over to do the same and saw that the number had been blocked.

"Excuse me," Burke said to Allie and the others.

With a pointed look to Eve that she interpreted as a bid to follow him, Burke walked away. In this, she and Burke were on the same page. Following him was exactly what Eve intended to do. "Sorry, Allie. Raincheck."

She fell into step with Burke as he wove his way through the men and women milling about the conference room and returned to the hotel lobby. Burke flipped open the phone but didn't put it to his ear. Eve leaned toward him and saw that the caller had sent a text message. The angle of the phone, though, prevented her from reading it. An instant later Burke closed the phone.

"Well?" Eve asked.

"I'm to check in then proceed to my room. Our caller will meet me there in ten minutes."

Eve felt excitement course through her.

Burke raised his gaze and his dark eyes settled on her. "If this is the buyer making contact, I'm wondering why he upped the time of the meeting and changed the location?"

Eve didn't care for the suspicion she heard in Burke's tone. "I have no answers for those questions and I'm not about to stand here with you and analyze his motives. As far as I'm concerned if this is the buyer or the accomplice, getting this over with now rather than later would be a good thing."

Burke did not respond to her comment. He used his own cell phone and placed a call. After a brief pause, he said, "Lanski. Change in plans." Burke went on to inform Lanski about the message he'd received then gave the order to mobilize a team of agents. "Tell our people to hold their positions. No one moves in without my order." Burke ended the call then turned to her. "Okay, Doctor, let's go."

Burke proceeded to the front desk with Eve in tow.

"I'd like to check in," he said to the young male clerk.

"Sure thing, sir." The clerk nodded, and the red and blue tints in his hair glittered in the light from the chandelier overhead. "Name please."

"Richard Patterson."

"Are you with the chemist's convention, sir?" he asked conversationally.

"Yes."

The young man tapped the computer keyboard. "A great line up of speakers this year."

"Quite good," Burke agreed.

"Here you are, Dr. Patterson." The clerk handed Burke a key card. "Room 1117 just like you asked for. Enjoy your stay."

Burke signed the register. "Thank you."

Burke and Eve left the desk and the clerk bent his head over a stack of papers. A woman rushed by them, bearing an armload of towels.

"Did Richard reserve this room in addition to arranging accommodation at the cottage?" Burke asked.

"I don't know. Can your people look into

that?"

"I'll get Lanski on it but since the room isn't billed until checkout, there's no way to trace the reservation through a credit card. I don't like going into this meeting blind."

Eve's stomach tensed. "We have no choice. We have to see this through and do as your caller instructed."

He studied her. "I have every intention of seeing this through."

With his hand at her back, Burke steered Eve to the bank of elevators. The lobby was quiet now. The chemist's conference was the big event at the hotel at this time of year and most of the hotel patrons were gathered in the conference room to hear Dr. Abernathy speak. No doubt Richard's buyer would have known that and choosing this meeting time when few people would be about had not been a coincidence.

Eve waited outside the room Burke had been assigned while he performed his customary check of the surroundings.

"All clear," he said a few moments later.

Eve joined him inside. He hung a "do not disturb" placard on the exterior door knob, which she figured he'd also been instructed by the caller to do.

The room was a suite and a large one with plush furnishings and gilt accessories. A bottle of champagne cooled in a silver ice bucket. Strawberry, mango, and kiwi from an abundant fruit basket scented the air. It was precisely the kind of accommodation Richard would have booked for himself. If she'd made the arrangements, she would have reserved a simple room for Richard, like one she'd book for herself.

"Why that look?" Burke asked.

Eve removed her gaze from the long hall that led to the bedroom and looked to Burke. "Just that this room is so typically Richard." She shrugged. "When he checked into a hotel, he always chose the best room available." She didn't add that he would have spared no expense if the business was paying. He had no concern for where the business stood financially. How many times had she gone head to head with him over expenses he charged to their partnership?

She shook off those irrelevant thoughts and directed her attention where it needed to be. "Is it possible the meeting at the cottage is a dupe and that this is the real meeting? That Richard and the buyer made a plan you don't know about? Could your Intel be off?"

"No."

Burke's firm tone left no doubt that he trusted his information. Eve accepted his word on that. She glanced at her watch. "It's been ten minutes."

Burke sat on the arm of the chesterfield. "Yeah."

Eve walked to a floor-to-ceiling window. The day had cleared. There wasn't a cloud visible now. Sunlight streamed in, bathing the room in its warm glow. The suite overlooked an enclosed garden. Flowers and shrubs were in full bloom. The view was breathtaking, but Eve was not in a frame of mind to appreciate it. She turned away to pace the room. Sixty minutes went by. She was wearing grooves in the rug, she thought.

Another hour later, she stopped in front of Burke. "He should have been here by now."

Burke nodded. "I think we can say whoever sent the message isn't coming."

Burke took out his phone and called Lanski. Eve tuned out Burke's voice as he told Lanski the meeting was a bust. Disappointment weighed on her.

"... a set up," Burke said, then ended the call.

His last words had caught her attention. "What did you mean a set up—set up for what?"

"That's what I'd like to know. Someone just played with us, Doctor. I'd like to know why."

She met his pointed stare. "Are you insinuating something?"

"Not insinuating. Asking outright. Did you set up this little diversion?"

"Why would I do that?"

"As a signal to the buyer that your plan has gone south?"

"A signal ..." Eve shook her head. "How could I have set this up?" She spread her arms wide. "I was with you when you got the cell phone text. I couldn't have sent that. I want this guy found more than you do. It's my life on the line if we don't."

"It's your life on the line if we do find him. Once we have the buyer, we'll have you. You won't be able to deny your involvement."

"I have nothing to deny."

They left the room and rode the elevator to the lobby in a stony silence. When the doors opened, Eve stepped out ahead of Burke.

"Eve!"

Allie stood at the door to the conference room, shoulders raised, gaze intent, frantically waving to her. Abernathy's lecture was over. Only a handful of people still lingered in the lobby and Eve crossed the room quickly to Allie.

"Eve, my dear," Allie said. "I'd almost despaired of seeing you again today."

Allie clutched her hand and Eve's fears for herself dimmed for the moment in the face of his distress. "What is it Allie? Are you all right?"

"Yes. Yes." He shook his head. A slight smile trembled on his thin lips. "Forgive me, my dear. Forgive my theatrics. You left in such a hurry that you forgot your handbag beneath the chair you'd been occupying." He held her cream-colored envelope purse aloft. "I hope you don't mind. I thought it best to retrieve it for you, rather than permit it to be placed in a lost and found." Allie blinked owl-like and eyed her expectantly, awaiting confirmation, it appeared to Eve, that he'd acted well.

Eve smiled. "Thank you. I did forget about getting my purse when I left the conference room."

"You dashed out in such a hurry, I feared you had taken ill?"

"No. I'm just fine."

Eve skirted Allie's implied question of where she went, and Allie didn't press her. His concern for her touched Eve. She reached out and hugged him. His arms closed gently around her. The contact filled with such genuine affection brought tears to Eve's eyes. Her current situation had her tense and on edge and she welcomed the comfort of a friend.

She hadn't realized how close to the edge she was until a sob shook her. Allie's hold on her tightened.

"There, there, my dear." Allie's voice softened. His tone became soothing. "Are you quite sure you're all right?"

Her emotions were out of proportion to Allie's act of retrieving her purse. Feeling embarrassed at almost blubbering on the man over a simple act of kindness, Eve pulled back from him.

"My life is in my purse," she said, invoking some humor to cover her embarrassment. "You saved me from having to deal with credit card companies and the DMV and a host of other bureaucrats."

Allie cast a narrow eyed glance at Burke. Eve wondered if Allie's matchmaking tendencies were kicking in and he was considering that Burke—ah, Richard—was responsible for her upset. She and Burke had left the lecture together, after all.

Burke showed no reaction to the animosity now coming off Allie in waves. Though Eve felt grateful for Allie's loyalty and his fierce protectiveness of her, she didn't want to cause her friend any further distress. She hurried to reassure him that she was well.

She gave him a bright smile. "Thank you, Allie. You saved the day." Allie was considerably shorter than she and Eve bent and gave him a kiss on his cheek.

The deep furrows cutting into Allie's brows eased. "Glad to have been of service. Now, will you do me the honor of accompanying me to an early dinner?" He rubbed his hands together. "I'm positively famished. I will also fill you in on the latter part of Dr. Abernathy's lecture. Fascinating. Positively fascinating the strides he's made."

It would be an early dinner. It was just minutes after three p.m. Eve was in no mood to sit down to a meal, less in the mood to hear about Abernathy's lecture. Her nerves were frazzled and she knew she wouldn't be able to keep up appearances for much longer. All she could think about was getting back to the cottage to lay in wait for the meeting at midnight.

She didn't know how Burke felt about Allie's invitation. Didn't know if Burke wanted to join Allie for a meal, maybe to keep up appearances. At the moment, she didn't care what Burke wanted. She was tired of having him decide her every movement for her. She simply wasn't up to any more pretense this day.

She turned to Allie and shook her head, "I'm sorry, Allie. Not tonight."

Without giving Burke a chance to refute her, she walked away.

* * *

He watched Eve Collins leave the conference. Head down she pushed through the double glass doors that led to the parking lot. The late afternoon breeze caught her hair and it swirled around her face.

Through the mass of dark strands, he saw that her features were pale and drawn. She looked "blown away". The joke provoked a chuckle.

Simply put, Eve looked blindsided by the situation she found herself in. Didn't know what hit her. As well she should. He had worked hard to orchestrate recent events.

Before anyone could speculate if Richard Patterson had been working alone, the man who now watched Eve had thought it prudent to provide a decoy. Who better for that role than Patterson's actual business partner? Eve had been the perfect choice. He laughed again.

There was no doubt about her guilt. His text message earlier to meet in a room in this hotel was icing on a very tall cake. When the buyer failed to attend the meeting, it appeared she had warned the buyer of the trap.

And now, with his anonymity assured, it was time he returned to the task at hand, obtaining the formula. He had taken steps to do that. It was just a matter of a little more time.

He could afford to be patient. Once the formula was sold, the hefty payoff would assure there wasn't anything he could not afford.

Eve Collins reached Richard Patterson's vehicle and got inside. Eyes narrowed now, his attention returned to her. Eve's role in his plan was almost complete. There was just one more thing for her to do and that was to die.

* * *

Burke was quiet on the drive back to the cottage. Eve welcomed his silence. She was too upset for conversation. With him for his refusal to consider her innocence. With this latest development in her situation.

Was it the buyer who'd contacted Burke? If so why hadn't he gone ahead to the hotel room? Had he stayed away because he discovered that his plan with Richard had gone wrong? She had no way of knowing. She did know that the failure of whoever had made contact to appear in Richard's hotel room had reinforced Burke's notion of her guilt.

Richard's accomplice had not shown up in the hotel room either. The one person she desperately needed to make an appearance. Was that because Richard hadn't been alive to let him know about the plan to meet at the hotel? That made sense since Richard was the contact to the buyer.

Eve released a frustrated breath and leaned back against the head rest. Round and round she went with no answers. Bottom line: the accomplice hadn't revealed himself which meant she was no closer to proving her innocence. Until she did, she would remain under suspicion of treason.

She shuddered. Frustration gave way to the true emotion driving her: fear.

Burke stopped at the restaurant they'd breakfasted at. While she waited in the car, he went inside. He returned with two take-out meals which he placed on the console. The aroma wafting from the containers revealed that he'd bought chicken.

At the cottage, Eve left the car, striding quickly over the mowed grass. She'd almost lost it with Allie. The last thing she wanted was to break down in front of Burke.

When he opened the door to the cottage, she moved to precede him inside. He clutched her arm, halting her.

Eve turned on him. "You think I have the buyer in here ready to spring an ambush on you?"

"I can't discount the possibility."

She didn't know if he was deliberately trying to bait her or truly believed what he said. "You're unbelievable."

"You want to know what I'm really thinking?" Burke crossed his arms. "Your buyer has gone to ground. He won't show for tonight's meeting either. He knows that this is a bust and he's better off to cut his losses and move on."

Burke's prediction sent a chill through her. "I hope you're wrong."

Burke's gaze hardened. "I hope so too, Doctor."

* * *

Burke confirmed that he and Eve were alone in the cottage. He needed to phone Lanski and went outside where the signal would be stronger for his cell phone.

The fresh air was welcome. He needed it to clear his head and cool his temper. He'd lost his temper with Dr. Collins. Again. Unheard of for him when dealing with suspects. He made sure to keep his emotions in check when on the job.

He wouldn't have to worry about her much longer. By this time tomorrow, whether or not they apprehended the buyer, she would be out of his life.

That thought didn't give him the satisfaction or pleasure that it should have.

Burke made the call to Lanski. Two rings later, his second in command picked up.

"Our people are in place, boss," Lanski said. "At your signal, we'll move in. We'll get the buyer when he shows."

Burke grunted. "If he shows."

"You don't think he will?"

Burke left the question unanswered. "There's been no activity from Dr. Collins's cell phone, I take it?"

"No, sir. I would have let you know immediately. I've been hoping that the lady doc might have named the buyer by now and we can just round him up."

"She's still saying she doesn't know what Patterson was up to. We know that Patterson never met his buyer, so we have no reason to think Dr. Collins would have. She doesn't know who is supposed to show up here tonight any more than we do."

"So she says."

"Something's not right," Burke said quietly.

"What do you mean?"

"This afternoon, if it was the buyer who contacted me, he didn't ask if I had the formula with me. He just went ahead and set up the meeting."

"An oversight? Or maybe he assumed Patterson would have it with him at all times."

"The people we're dealing with don't leave things to chance. This guy would *make* sure."

"Maybe he realized that he hadn't confirmed you had the formula and that's why he blew off the meet."

"No." Burke shook his head. "This guy has been on the ball since the start of this."

"Dr. Collins must have tipped him off somehow."

"That was my first thought." Burke narrowed his gaze at a squirrel perched high on a tree limb. "Now, I'm not sure. Since he didn't ask about the formula, makes me think it wasn't the buyer at all. That we have another player in this game."

"Doesn't sound likely."

"Something else is going on here. I don't know what." Burke didn't add that the not knowing had his stomach churning. "The buyer doesn't want to play games. He wants to do business. What happened today wasn't about getting the formula."

* * *

The midnight hour came and went. Eve stood waiting for a knock on the cottage door that did not come. Burke had been right. The buyer was a no-show.

Still when he said it aloud, the words struck Eve hard. "So what are you going to do about that?" she asked. "All right, the buyer hasn't shown himself. Fine." Eve flung her arms out from her sides. "Onto Plan 'B'."

He turned from the window to face her. "There is no Plan 'B'."

"Then let's come up with one. Maybe you

weren't convincing as Richard and your cover was blown. Maybe the buyer and accomplice were tipped off. If so, we need to find out who did that."

Burke gave her a steady look.

"You can't still be thinking that I alerted anyone because if you are—"

"It doesn't matter at this point." Burke loosened his tie, the movement jerky, laced with anger, belying his words.

"What do you mean it doesn't matter. This guy poses a threat to our security and you're just going to let him go? Just like that?"

Burke went still and his gaze bore into hers. "Oh, we're not going to let him go. Make no mistake about that. We will continue to search for the buyer. You, however, will no longer be involved in the search."

Eve's stomach plummeted. "So this is it? You're now going to send me to Washington where I'll be charged?"

"I'm not going to send you. I'm going to escort you. And, yeah, you'll now have to answer to the claims against you. Get yourself a good defense lawyer, Doctor, you can play this out in the courts for years."

Years. She could be in custody or with her life on hold for years.

"That's unacceptable, Burke. I'm not ready to give up looking for Richard's accomplice."

"Well, you can hire investigators to do your digging for you through your lawyer. We'll be leaving for Washington in the morning."

Eve shivered. She could see there was no way

to convince him otherwise. It was over. Just what the government had to make a charge of treason stick, she didn't know, but would soon find out.

The cottage suddenly felt stifling. Eve went to the door.

"Where are you going?" Burke asked.

"Outside," she said and before he could ask anything further, hurried out.

Would he follow her? She was in his custody, after all. But, when he didn't she figured he must have reasoned, just where would she go? The cottage delivered on its promise of seclusion. She'd never find the road on foot at night and Burke had the keys to Richard's car. Eve closed her eyes, fighting despair. She wrapped her arms tight around herself and headed for a small stand of trees and shrubs that made up a garden.

A scattering of stars and a quarter moon lit her path. She still wore the suit and strappy sandals she'd put on for the conference and the shorn grass chilled her bare feet.

A wooden swing was placed among the trees. As she approached it, she was grabbed from behind.

CHAPTER FIVE

A large hand closed over Eve's mouth. An arm wrapped around her waist, scooping her off her feet.

She fought panic, and stiffening her elbow, reared back, striking her captor in the sternum. He let out a whoosh of air and released her. She turned toward her attacker, prepared to deliver another blow, then stopped.

"Matt?"

"Eve." He paused for breath. "Sorry, I didn't mean to scare you." Another pause. "Did I hurt you?"

Since he was the one on his knees in the grass, clutching his chest, the question seemed ridiculous.

"Matt, what are you doing here? How did you find me?"

He held up a hand, the large hand that an instant earlier had covered her mouth and she saw that the metal she'd felt against her lips was a class ring.

"I'll explain. Just let me get my wind back." He exhaled a breath that wheezed. "Hot damn, woman, you pack a punch." One side of his moustache lifted in a smile.

Eve wasn't in the mood for his charm. "I'd like some answers, Matt."

He sat back on his haunches and jerked his tie until it hung below his breast bone. It occurred to Eve that for a large man he couldn't take a hit well.

"It's like this," he said slowly. "I got worried about you when you ran out of Abernathy's lecture today. I did some checking. Found out that you weren't registered at the hotel. Allie remembered that you mentioned you were staying at a cottage in the county. I got the address from him."

"And just why did you do that?" Burke asked. His tone was lethal.

Eve hadn't heard Burke approach. At the sound of his voice, she whirled around. He was now standing behind her.

Deligne got slowly to his feet. His eyes sharpened on Burke and Eve saw that he, too, had registered a threat from Burke. Judging the speed she'd taken Matt down, Burke would wipe the ground with the chemist. Matt stood no chance against him. She couldn't let Matt be hurt.

She faced Matt, giving Burke her back again, and remaining between the two men. Burke gripped her forearm and moved her behind him.

"I already told Eve," Matt said. "Maybe you missed it. I got worried about her when she ran out of Abernathy's lecture today. With you, Rick. And didn't come back."

Eve stepped out from behind Burke. "I didn't tell Allie where I was staying, Matt."

Matt met her gaze and held it for a heartbeat, then exhaled deeply. He winced and ran his hand back through his hair. "Okay. Truth time."

His Stetson lay in the dirt. He bent to retrieve it, then struck it against the leg of his jeans. A puff of dirt rose in the air. He placed the hat carefully on the wooden swing behind him.

"I tracked you because I've been keeping you under surveillance, Eve," Deligne said. "I'm not a Texas rancher. I'm with British Intelligence."

Gone was the Texas drawl, replaced by an aristocratic British accent. Eve sucked in a breath. Burke's gaze narrowed further.

"We know about the formula," Deligne went on. "And we know that Richard Patterson is dead." Deligne looked pointedly at Burke. "So just who the hell are you, mate?"

When Burke didn't respond, Eve said, "John Burke. He's with a covert department of the CIA."

"American Intelligence." Deligne nodded. "I should have guessed that."

"A spy, Matt?" Eve asked. "You've been spying on me?"

"Couldn't be helped, love," he said softly. "My orders were to secure the formula and to bring both you and Richard in. I fought the order about you. I know you're not a terrorist, Eve." His jaw tightened. "I planned to confront Patterson about that when he showed up at the hotel. To beat the fact that he lied about your involvement out of him." Deligne's gaze shone with conviction.

Eve felt lightheaded at the thought that someone believed in her innocence. Matt couldn't know what his words meant to her, especially now, on this night. Her throat clogged with tears and for a moment she couldn't speak. She swallowed then said, "Thank you for believing in me."

Matt focused on her. He reached out slowly and touched her wrist. "No need to thank me. I could no more doubt your innocence than I could my own. I care mightily for you, Eve. I've made no secret of it. I've cared for you long before you became an assignment. When we were just two chemists talking shop." He smiled. "It was talking with you, being with you that drew me to this conference every year. It can't come as much of a surprise to you that I made the trip every year to see you, Eve."

"Very touching," Burke said. "What do you know about a meeting between Patterson, Eve, and the buyer that was scheduled for tonight?"

Red spread across Deligne's cheeks. His jaw tightened and he remained silent.

"You don't have a problem answering my questions do you, Deligne?" Burke crossed his arms. "Seeing that you care mightily for Eve?" Burke's tone was thick with sarcasm.

Deligne met Burke's gaze. "I know all about the meeting and that whoever was supposed to make an appearance to purchase the formula did not."

"And what do you know about our guy failing to show up?" Burke said.

Deligne sidestepped Eve and moved to Burke.

His gaze hardened. "Have you not heard one word I've said? I did not give myself away. I want Eve's innocence proven, so I would not risk a chance to do that. I am very good at what I do. I was not detected. I am not the reason the buyer knew not to come here tonight. I am as disappointed as you are at the outcome of this event." Deligne's lips curled in an expression of disgust. "That said, however, what's done cannot be undone. Listen to me, mate. My government wants the same things yours wants—the formula secured and the buyer apprehended. I propose that we work together to that end."

Burke kept his gaze on Deligne, watching the man steadily. "A partnership? You're proposing a partnership between our two agencies. Between you and I?"

Matt's face tightened in what looked like annoyance at Burke's comment. "We both want the same things. An exchange of information, an agreement to keep each other in the loop would benefit us both and prevent us from treading over the same ground."

Burke's cell phone rang. He glanced at the screen then stepped away to take the call. Eve watched him. He walked until he was almost to the cottage. There he stopped and put the phone to his ear. She could not hear his conversation which was obviously as he'd intended.

Regardless, her gaze and her attention remained focused on Burke. Whatever Matt was presently saying didn't register. Her attention was on Burke. Was his caller Lanski? Since Burke was frowning, did that mean he'd received bad news?

Though, as she considered that—she was suspected of treason—the appointment to find Richard's accomplice, the one man who could prove her innocence, was a bust. Really, how much worse could the situation get?

"Eve, we need to get you out of this mess."

Eve forced her gaze from Burke and focused on Matt. "I couldn't agree with you more. The question is how."

"I have some ideas about that."

Her pulse picked up. "I'd love to hear them. At the moment, I'm fresh out and Burke is content to take me to Washington in the morning and let me take my chances with the government."

"Yes, well, it isn't his life on the line is it?" Matt's mouth tightened briefly. "Once he delivers the formula, and you to his superiors, his job is done. To him, you are no more than an assignment. Your fate means nothing to him."

Eve could not deny that.

"I can't stand that you're being persecuted," Matt said. "What you're facing is killing me, Eve. I can't do a thing about it. We don't have any proof and we have no leads to getting any."

"But you said—"

He looked up at the stars and shook his head sadly. "I know what I said. All a bluff. The truth is all evidence points to you and Patterson. With Patterson now unable to refute his claim and exonerate you, you alone are here to face prosecution." He made a sound of disgust. "My government feels the same way as yours. You're guilty in the eyes of my superiors and my orders are to prevent you from selling the formula. Even if that means using deadly force." He released a deep breath and said softly. "I would more easily use deadly force on myself." His eyes lowered to hers. Very slowly his hand came up to stroke her chin. "In case you haven't guessed it by now, I'm in love with you, Eve. There, I've said it. It feels good to finally get that out in the open."

Eve forced herself not to pull back from Matt's touch. He was an attractive man. A handsome man. But he did nothing for her. Since Emily's death and the break up of her marriage, no man had attracted her. Her gaze strayed to Burke.

She returned her attention to Matt. "Matt..."

"Oh, I know you don't return my feelings, but that doesn't seem to matter. I feel what I feel."

Eve didn't know how to respond to that.

"Eve, listen to me." Matt's tone grew urgent. "Burke won't lay it all out for you. He wants you cooperative and easy to manage. If we don't do something, he'll manage you right into a prison cell. The truth of your situation is that you'll die in prison, if you aren't executed first. We have to get away from here. Go somewhere we can't be found."

"Matt, what are you talking about? What about your government? Your life. You can't just disappear. You don't want to disappear—"

"To hell with my government. Do you think I can hand you over?" His features tightened as his expression grew fierce. "And about my life—I want my life with you. Yes, I can and will disappear. I will disappear with you. To keep you safe. I will disappear with you."

"Matt, I can't live like that, and you can't

either. I need to prove my innocence."

"Darling Eve." He gripped her shoulders. "My government and yours are building a case against you. They don't care if you're innocent. They want someone to take the fall—a scapegoat to present to the media and to the British and American public to assure them that our national security is safe and that the government is doing its job. You fit the bill. No one is seeking to prove your innocence. Surely, not Burke's people. Not Burke. Your only chance is to come away with me."

"Matt—"

"You're being hunted by our two governments. We need to disappear, but before we do, we must destroy the formula. The world doesn't need another method to kill. We must destroy the formula, if it's still accessible." Matt's tone sharpened and he stared at Eve without blinking. "Has Burke turned it in to his superiors?"

Eve rubbed her brow. "I don't think so."

Matt's grip on her dug into her skin. "Where is he keeping it?"

"I never asked, not that he would have told me." Eve shook her head. "I don't know where it is."

"Okay. We need to find it. The most important thing is that Burke still has it." Matt eased his grip on her.

"The formula is safe with Burke," Eve said. "I believe that he will do the right thing with it."

Deligne sneered. "Burke will turn it in to his government where it will be a threat to us all. We aren't too late to remove that threat. My final act for my country is going to be to destroy this weapon. Then you and I will go somewhere we can't be found."

"Matt—"

He pressed his fingers to her lips. "Think about it. But think quickly. You said Burke is taking you to Washington. Time is running out. Once you're in Washington, we won't be able to get away. It will be too late."

* * *

Lanski's surveillance of the cottage had observed Deligne and identified the chemist. As Burke spoke with his second in command, he continued to watch Eve and Deligne.

"What do you want me to do about him?" Lanski asked now. "You want Deligne picked up when he leaves you?"

"No. Run a check on him."

"We checked all of the chemists, Deligne included. He's clean."

"This time, go deep. Deligne claims he's with British Intelligence. I want his identity confirmed and right away."

"I'll get right on it. What about now? You want me to keep our people in place?"

"Call them off," Burke said. "It's over."

"You sure about that? Even about Deligne? If he turns out to be a phony, you're on your own. We don't know who else he may decide to call. You'll have no back up, boss."

"No. Go. I don't want to spook Deligne if he

turns out to be other than who he claims. We need a break in this case. Deligne just may be that break."

"You don't believe he's who he says?"

"That's what I want to find out," Burke said carefully.

"We can take him in for questioning?"

"No point to that. We have nothing on him. I want him free to make a move, if he's going to. Put a tail on him—a loose tail. Let's see where he goes. Who he talks to."

"I'll be in touch," Lanski said.

Burke ended the call. He'd deliberately stepped away to take Lanski's call, though, speaking with the agent could have waited until he'd finished speaking with Deligne. The investigation was going nowhere fast, however, and Burke had decided to step away, to leave Deligne and Eve alone, to give them privacy to make a move, or plan one, if they intended to.

So far all Deligne had done was fawn all over Eve. Burke scowled at the thought. He didn't trust Eve. He certainly didn't trust Deligne. For all he knew, the man claiming to be an intelligence agent was as involved with the formula as she and Patterson were. And, there was still the matter of just how Richard Patterson died.

Deligne gave Eve a mega-watt smile. His interest in Eve was not Burke's business unless it pertained to the investigation. But when Deligne's hand moved to Eve's cheek, Burke's scowl deepened.

* * *

"I can't go with you, Matt," Eve said.

Matt shook his head slowly. "You're making a mistake."

"I have to clear my name. I'm innocent. I can't live the rest of my life on the run." She'd be damned if she'd run, if she'd let her life be stolen from her. *Not without a fight.* She lifted her chin. "I won't go with you, Matt. Thank you for believing in me."

Matt lifted a shoulder, let it fall. "That's it then. You'll be in Washington by this time tomorrow."

Eve said nothing.

Matt bent toward her and kissed her cheek. Then he left.

Eve hugged herself against a sudden chill as her bravado deserted her. The one person who'd believed in her innocence was gone and she was now completely alone.

* * *

Burke was awake on the sofa in the cottage, watching Eve through the window, when the call came in from Lanski. Deligne had left some time ago. She'd moved to the garden swing and had been sitting there ever since.

"Hey," Lanski said. "Got the check you wanted on Deligne."

"Hold on."

Lanski's voice was breaking up. Burke tossed back the blanket, got to his feet, and made his way outside. The air was chill and dressed in jeans, T-shirt and no socks, it raised gooseflesh. A couple of mosquitoes took an interest in him, drawn to the glow coming off the panel of his cell phone. Burke swatted them away.

Keeping his gaze on Eve, Burke said, "Go ahead, Lanski. What did you find out?"

"Our sources confirmed he's legit. Deligne is with British Intelligence. He's also a chemist and his specialty is chemical weapons terrorism. He's the British version of you, Burke."

Burke grunted at that. "Anything else?"

"On a personal level he's single. No kids. No ex-wives. He could be a poster boy for Queen and Country, he's so clean."

Burke's lips thinned. "Okay. Thanks."

"Do you want us to call off our surveillance on him?"

"Yeah."

Burke ended the call as Eve returned to the cabin. She stopped in front of him.

"I need to tell you one last time that I am innocent," she said. "You are making a mistake."

Burke watched her, standing proudly before him, shoulders erect, chin uplifted, as she repeated her claim of innocence. Beneath it all, though, there was fear in her eyes. He didn't like seeing it. Didn't like knowing she was afraid.

She was a traitor. She had devised a weapon that would kill innocents for her own profit. She didn't deserve his compassion. He hardened his heart against her plea.

"If I had a dollar for every time I've heard that from a suspect," he said. "I wouldn't be working for Uncle Sam."

Burke brushed by her and entered the cottage,

leaving her standing in the doorway, alone.

CHAPTER SIX

Inside her bedroom, Eve sat on the end of the bed. There would be no help from Burke. What was she going to do?

She could understand his need to do his job and apprehend the terrorist, but couldn't he see that she wasn't a terrorist? Richard had been on his own in this. She had nothing to do with it. How was she going to prove her innocence if she was in custody in Washington? She would hire a lawyer of course, but she had little faith and less liking for lawyers, a left-over dislike from her days on the LAPD, she supposed.

She needed to remain in the field—hunting the buyer herself—which wasn't going to happen if she went to Washington in the morning. She went to her purse and removed the pen injector that contained her regular insulin. It was time for her last shot of the day. She needed this shot. She wasn't feeling at top form. No doubt the stress of the situation she was in and her constant sparring with Burke were depleting her strength. She always took great care to keep her sugar levels balanced. Her health was not something she took for granted.

At the moment, though, her hand was slick with sweat brought on by the disappointment that the accomplice and buyer hadn't shown up and by her frustration with Burke. If she didn't focus, she would break the tip of the needle in her arm. Inhale. Deeply. Exhale. Slowly.

She swabbed a spot on her upper arm. She always aimed for a spot that was more fleshy than muscle, but missed this time and a drop of blood beaded at the insertion point. She hissed in her breath. She swabbed alcohol onto the spot again, which startled another gasp out of her then fumbled with a bandage.

She changed out of her tan slacks and coral blouse and slipped on one of the lightweight night shirts she'd packed. The cool crisp cotton, in a powder blue, was sleeveless and grazed her knees. She was tired. It had been a long and disappointing day. She really needed to lie down.

On the bed, sweat broke out on her forehead, and trickled down the side of her face. Her next breath was fast and hard to take. The green lilies patterned on the bedspread swam out of focus. She must be more tired than she realized and rubbed her eyes, then the back of her neck.

Her hand fell away from her neck and dropped to her side. A feeling of lethargy overcame her. Her eyes drifted closed. She forced them open. Something was very wrong. Eve called out to Burke. He was in the next room and would surely hear her, but when she uttered his name, it was a feeble whisper that she barely heard herself.

She told herself to stand but only managed to lift her head and shoulders for an instant before crumpling back onto the mattress. She needed help. Her room wasn't equipped with a phone, but her cell phone was in her purse which she'd left on the bed. At the moment, the bag looked an ocean away.

The perspiration on her skin cooled and she shivered. Her teeth chattered. She raised her arm. Numbness was spreading through her body and her arm felt like a lead weight as she dragged it across the mattress. She clawed at the flap of her purse. Finally, the snap gave way. She probed inside and in slow, jerky movements yanked out her phone. Her fingers felt as thick as sausages as she pressed the 'talk" button and then jabbed the buttons 9-1-1.

"Emergency," a female operator said.

Eve's lips felt numb and barely moved as she mumbled a garbled, "Help," in a voice that was a croak.

Her eyelids drooped. She forced them open. Her vision blurred and the light dimmed. What happened to the light? She realized her vision was fading. No ... No! She screamed the denial yet she made no sound.

She struggled to lift herself off the mattress and gain her feet. Perspiration popped out on her forehead with the strain, yet she didn't move.

Her eyes closed. Her fingers went slack. She lost her grip on the phone and it struck the plank flooring with a dull thud. Eve didn't hear it.

* * *

Eve opened her eyes. She squinted at the sudden brightness that hurt and groaned. She raised her arm to fend off the intrusive light. Something was attached to her wrist.

"Easy."

The low male voice was Burke's.

"Light hurting your eyes?" he asked softly.

It felt as if she were being nicked by tiny knives. Eve mumbled an acknowledgment and the light dimmed.

The pain receded to a dull headache. She exhaled deeply.

In the soft glow of the overhead light, she saw she was in a bed, but not the bed at the cottage. This one had the chrome rails of a hospital bed. She was in a cubicle, now enclosed by a white curtain. Burke stood at the side of the bed. His deep-set gaze was fixed on her.

"Where am I?" she asked.

"You're in St. Mary's Hospital in Rowland County. How do you feel?"

She gave a non-committal grunt that had Burke's brows drawing together.

"What happened?" She raised her arm, this time to swat away hair that had fallen across her eyes, and was again stopped by what she now saw was an IV line.

Burke reached out and gently brushed the hair back from her face with his knuckles. "You collapsed at the cottage. That's all I've been told so far. A nurse took blood and ran some tests.

We're waiting for the results."

Eve frowned taking in Burke's words. The last thing she remembered was reaching for her cell phone.

"Sounds like I was lucky that you found me and got me here."

Burke shook his head. "I didn't find you. An ambulance showed up at the cottage and the paramedics told me they'd received a distress call from that location. I didn't have anything to do with getting you here. You saved yourself, Eve."

She couldn't remember placing the call. The curtain shifted and a tall pear-shaped man in his middle fifties entered the cubicle. His skin was a warm brown.

"I am Dr. Malhi." He smiled, exposing a crooked incisor and glanced from Eve to Burke, including him in the introduction. "I am heartened to see you have awakened."

"Can you tell me what happened, Doctor?" Eve asked.

"We have only just received your test results. The blood work it has indicated that your blood sugar was extremely low. Has your prescription insulin recently been changed?"

"No."

"How often do you take insulin injections?"

"Three times a day."

"Have you ever experienced a similar reaction?"

"No."

"Paramedics retrieved your insulin medication and brought it here to the hospital. I see that you are taking a rapid-acting insulin and a regular-acting insulin."

"Yes."

"The rapid acting insulin is only for your daytime use. It appears that you administered the rapid-acting insulin a short while ago, rather than the regular insulin. Doing so will lower blood glucose considerably and is likely to trigger the kind of episode you just experienced. This is not a mistake to be made lightly. Severe hypoglycaemia as you experienced can cause cardiac arrhythmia. Frankly, you are most fortunate that this mistake has not cost you your life."

"I did not take the wrong insulin, Doctor. I know the risks and I'm very careful about my medication."

"That is not what your blood has told us Ms. Collins. When we examined your insulin medication, we learned that the insulin bottles in the injectors did not match their prescription labels. It appears that when you replenished your insulin, you placed the rapid acting insulin in the injector labeled with the prescription for the regular insulin and vice versa. We have corrected the error. You are very fortunate, indeed, that all has turned out well."

Eve frowned. "That's impossible. I've been using those injectors for a while. I have not changed the bottles recently."

Malhi gave her a look that spoke plainly of his doubt. "I would like you to remain with us this night. If you are feeling well in the morning, you will be free to go home with your husband."

Malhi glanced at Burke who nodded. Eve supposed there was no point in clearing up

Malhi's mistake. It hardly seemed preferable to inform the doctor that she was Burke's charge, soon to be his prisoner.

She'd collapsed from an injection of rapid-acting insulin, Malhi said. Her insulin pen injectors were clearly labeled so she knew which was her night time insulin. When she replaced an empty bottle, she always checked the labels on the new bottle and on the injector to be sure they matched. *Always.* She would not make a mistake like that.

After Malhi left, Eve turned to Burke. "My collapse was not due to negligence. I don't take risks when it comes to my disease."

"You've been under a lot of stress lately. Do you not think it could be possible that you picked up the wrong injector tonight?"

No she did not think that was possible, but what other explanation was there?

* * *

The next morning, when she awoke, Burke was seated at her bedside. He was awake, watching her. If he'd feared her skipping out on him, he'd spent a night in that chair for nothing. There had been no chance of that happening. Last night, she'd felt too weak to sit up, let alone make a run for it.

Burke leaned toward her. "How do you feel?" His tone was gentle.

"Better."

A nurse entered the room. She eased around Burke, and applied a blood pressure cuff to Eve's arm.

"Doctor will be in to examine you shortly," the nurse said.

"I'll be outside," Burke said. He rubbed his hands down his face then got to his feet and started for the door.

Eve hadn't removed her suitcase from the trunk of Richard's car yet and she needed to change out of the hospital gown. "I could use my suitcase," Eve said to Burke. "It's in the trunk of the car. Would you?"

Burke nodded. "Be right back."

An hour later, Eve was discharged.

"Do you need anything before we return to the cottage?" Burke asked as he drove away from the hospital. "Something for your condition?" He shrugged, a gesture of helplessness that she didn't think he made often and one that he didn't appear comfortable with.

Eve appreciated the offer but shook her head. "I'm fine. Back to my usual self."

They drove the rest of the way back to the cottage in silence. Burke had the radio on low. A talk show host was bemoaning the state of the economy and an irate caller was blaming politicians for the problem. Eve tuned out the pair as they engaged in a lively debate over the issue and turned her attention out of the window. They were driving through a residential neighborhood. Lawns were neatly cut. Flowers were in full bloom. The air conditioning was on in the car, but Eve's nostrils flared slightly as she imagined she could smell the honeysuckle on a bush as the car streaked by it. If she didn't find out who Richard's accomplice was, it would be a very long time before she smelled honeysuckle again. Her shoulders slumped slightly with the thought and she resolutely straightened her posture. She was innocent. And she would prove that.

Burke parked in front of the cottage. They made their way to the front door. He inserted the key then pushed the door open. Eve waited, remaining in place so he could go inside first and conduct his usual check of the place. Burke gripped her elbow. There was a tension in him that hadn't been present a moment ago. Eve didn't know what had alerted or alarmed him, but there was no doubt that something had. She felt a rush of adrenaline. A fine sweat broke out on her body and the slight breeze that stirred the air as it blew across her arms, chilled her. When she glanced up at him, he shook his head, and removed his weapon from the shoulder holster he wore.

He entered the cottage.

She waited in a state of tension herself for a few moments that felt like hours when Burke appeared in the door way again.

"All clear," he said.

Eve followed him into the livingroom. "What made you think it wasn't going to be?"

"When I turned the key in the lock, there was no resistance. The door wasn't locked."

"Maybe you just forgot to lock it last night when you left here." Eve tossed back at him that maybe he'd been careless and left the door unlocked, as he'd suggested to her last night about her insulin injection.

Burke nodded. “Maybe.”

His easy acceptance and capitulation rang false. What he was hiding? “You don’t believe that, why not?”

Burke holstered his weapon, hesitated, then said, “Things have been moved. Examined.”

“Like?”

“Those books.”

He indicated a short shelf built into the wall by a small fireplace. She didn’t notice anything off about them.

“The pictures on the walls have been touched,” Burke went on quietly, his tone contemplative.

The three photos. Sure. She’d noticed them upon their arrival at the cottage, on the wall behind a bamboo couch covered with bright floral cushions. The pictures were photographs of nature scenes hung in a row. All were perfectly aligned.

Eve was about to question Burke about his belief that the photos had been touched but instead narrowed her eyes. One of the pictures—a photograph of a bird about to take flight—had been askew when they’d arrived here yesterday. It wasn’t now. There was no housekeeping service with the rental of the cottage, so no one had been in to clean and righted the picture.

Burke took his cell phone from his pocket and pressed a button with his thumb. As he raised the phone to his ear, he left the cottage to stand outside. Whether he didn’t want her to overhear his conversation or was just seeking some fresh air, Eve didn't know. Whatever, she would not be left out. She was in the unfortunate position of having her future tied with his and for the moment, she would allow him no secrets, if she could help it. She followed him outside.

"… yeah, Lanski," Burke said.

He didn't glance at her as she approached him, just went on speaking. Eve felt a little relief that he hadn't been attempting to exclude her from this conversation.

"She's fine."

Burke's gaze cut to her briefly and Eve figured he'd brought Lanski up to speed on her night at the hospital. He went on to inform Lanski about the search of the cottage.

"Whoever it was had to be looking for the formula," Burke said.

Eve's heart pounded. "Did he get it?"

Burke's gaze met hers. He shook his head.

Eve closed her eyes briefly, relieved that the deadly weapon was not at large.

"No," Burke said. "I'm going to bring her in today as planned. See you in Washington."

Eve's stomach fluttered. "That's it? Even after someone searched the cottage your part in finding the accomplice is over?"

Burke closed the lid of the cell phone. "That's it. The search yielded nothing since I have the formula and, as I already told you, we already have the accomplice."

"You're wrong."

Burke said nothing to her denial. "Get ready to travel, Doctor. We have a plane to catch."

Eve left Burke outside and went to her room.

Sunlight slanted across the unmade bed through a separation in the lavender curtains. Her purse and its contents, lipstick, compact, and wallet were strewn on the bunched bedspread. Her cell phone lay open on the thick area rug beside the bed. She picked up all of the items and replaced them in her purse.

Dr. Malhi had returned the pen injectors from yesterday. She wasn't due for another shot for a while and stuck both injectors in her purse.

Before she left, she wanted a shower. She suspected that once she arrived in Washington, she'd be whisked away to answer questions and a shower for her wouldn't be a priority for the government interrogators.

There was no point bringing her suitcase in from the car. The tan slacks and cream silk blouse she now wore would do for the trip. She scooped her dryer from the top of the dresser where she'd left it after having used it yesterday and went into the bathroom.

She undressed, placed the items on the solid gray counter, then reached into the shower stall and twisted the faucets. After a moment, she stepped beneath the hot spray.

She scrubbed, more vigorously than was needed, her movements fueled by frustration and fear at the situation she found herself in.

Finished with the shower, Eve gave the taps a sharp turn, shutting off the water, then emerged from the tub. She wrapped a towel around her hair, turban style, then another around her body, knotting it under her arm. She plugged in the hair dryer then sighed. She'd forgotten a comb.

The towel covered her from underarms to mid thigh. She didn't think Burke would go into shock if he glimpsed her in nothing more than the towel on the way to her bedroom. Besides, he might still be outside.

She left the bathroom. She was in the hall when something in that room exploded.

Eve screamed as the impact knocked her off her feet. Debris blew out of the room. She covered her head with her arms, but she was far enough that nothing struck her. She glanced back over her shoulder at the room she'd just vacated. Flames climbed the walls and spread along the bathroom vanity.

Eve was shaking. She didn't think her legs would support her were she to try to stand. Remaining on her hands and knees, she crawled across the floor.

Black smoke billowed into the room making it impossible to see her path to the front door. Her shoulder struck something—the leg of an end table she realized. Ignoring the throbbing pain in her arm, she veered away from the table. She had to slow down—calm down or she wouldn't make it out of there. When she would have scrambled forward, she forced herself to slow her pace, but her heart was pounding like a jackhammer.

The air, thick with smoke, choked her and set off a fit of coughing. Eve lowered her head as close to the floor as she could where the air was fresher. It was only marginally fresher and the lack of oxygen was getting to her. She felt light headed and spots danced before her eyes. She shook her head in an attempt to clear it but the spots remained. Smoke burned her eyes and they ran with tears.

She felt a blast of heat from behind her. She glanced over her shoulder. The fire had spread from the bathroom and flared on the walls in the room she was now in. A support post was now aflame and shrinking to kindling.

Very soon now the cottage would be engulfed. Her throat closed and fear brought fresh tears to her eyes. She fought the urge to continue to watch the flames—to mark the progress as the fire gained on her—and returned her attention to getting out.

The smoke thickened. Eve squinted, but she'd lost her bearings and didn't know just where she was in the cottage. Cold sweat drenched her. She was no longer sure if she was heading for the door—or to one of the walls. She would end up trapped if she went the wrong way ... Eve shuddered.

The front door was flung open. Sunlight flooded the room, illuminating Burke as he ran toward her.

"Eve!"

Her throat had closed and she couldn't answer him.

Burke dropped to his knees beside her. "Are you hurt?"

His gaze and his hands traveled up and down her body, concern and fear in his eyes as he checked her for injury. She was unhurt and as he realized that for himself, he wrapped his arm around her waist and hauled her to her feet. Her legs wobbled and he swung her up into his arms.

Eve wrapped her arms around his neck and holding her tight against his chest, Burke carried her out of the cottage. He lowered her onto the lawn, then ran back inside.

The fire had not yet spread to the front of the small accommodation, still, it was dangerous to go back inside. What was the man thinking?

"Burke," Eve tried to call out to him, but his name came out as a croak.

He was back quickly. Her purse was gripped in his fist. He'd gone back inside for her purse? Eve shook her head, unable to discern his logic.

His arm went around her again, and again he brought her to her feet. She thought he was looking to put additional distance between them and the cottage. Instead, he began to rub her arms gently.

"You're shivering." He removed his suit jacket. "We need to get you warm."

Her arms didn't seem to want to cooperate with her. He lifted them himself and slid them through the sleeves. He buttoned the jacket for her. He was a tall man. The sleeves covered her finger tips and the hem fell almost to her knees.

Eve cleared her throat. "Burke, we need to call 911. The fire will spread—"

Her teeth chattered which got her another worried look from Burke. He steered her to the car, opened the passenger side door and eased her down onto the seat. He swung her legs in himself and slammed the door.

"What are you doing?" Eve asked then repeated when he slid behind the steering wheel.

"Getting you out of here."

"Can't Washington wait until we've called for help?"

He didn't respond to her question and asked instead. "Do you need an insulin injection?"

"What?"

"Insulin. Do you need a shot now?"

She shook her head. He tossed her purse onto the console and she realized why he'd gone back into the cottage to retrieve it.

"Thank you," she said quietly.

He gave her a long look then nodded. He started the car. The engine roared to life. He switched from air conditioning to heat and aimed the vents at her. Eve huddled in his jacket and moved as close to the vents as the seat belt allowed.

Smoke rose from the cottage. Flames licked the roof. The fire was spreading fast.

"Burke, make the call. Alert Emergency Services of a gas leak."

"That explosion wasn't caused by a gas leak."

"What then?"

"A bomb."

"A bomb? What?"

"I found this in the hall." Burke took out a square of black plastic from his pocket and held it for her to see.

"It looks like it came from my hair dryer. What's that attached to it?"

"Part of a bomb casing. Someone wants you dead, Doctor."

CHAPTER SEVEN

Burke sped away from the cottage. He glanced at Eve, seated next to him. Her face was pale, her eyes huge with disbelief and fear. Her hands, tightly clasped together trembled. If he looked at his own hands, he'd likely find them in the same condition. When the bomb went off with her inside, he ran into the cottage like a mad man. He'd been crazed to get to her, fearing he'd find her dead. A tremor went through him at the memory. When he'd finally reached her, and had her in his arms, he'd wanted to hold her there where he knew she'd be safe.

What the hell was wrong with him? His grip on the steering wheel tightened in self-directed anger. Despite her claims of innocence, everything he knew about her told him she was a traitor to her country. Richard Patterson had named her in the terrorist plot. She was a woman who would murder innocents for her own gain without a qualm.

She was everything Burke loathed and risked his life to take down. She wasn't deserving of any tender feelings. If given the chance, he had no doubt she would take him out. There was the plain truth. He wouldn't lose sight of it again.

* * *

"My cell phone is in the inside pocket in my jacket. Hand it to me, would you?" Burke said.

They'd been quiet for a few moments, each lost in their own thoughts as Richard's car took them to Burke's destination and his voice startled her.

"What?"

"My phone. Inside pocket of my jacket."

Eve retrieved the phone and held it out. While he called emergency services about the fire, Eve took in what had just happened. Her hair dryer had been rigged with a bomb.

Burke completed the call, then made another. "I need a car." He leaned across Eve and withdrew a map from the glove box. "I'll be on Quarry Edge Road in fifteen minutes." He ended the call then set the phone on the console where he'd tossed her purse.

"Someone just tried to kill me," Eve said in a whisper.

A muscle in Burke's jaw pulsed.

The heat blasting from the vents had warmed her, but Eve shivered at the notion that someone wanted her dead.

Burke turned off Main Street onto an unpaved road. They were the only travelers on this road at the moment. He drove a short distance then came to a stop beside another vehicle, a white sedan that looked to be several years old.

Eve turned off the heat. "Why did you stop here?"

"Our new wheels, Doctor."

Burke left the vehicle, went around to the trunk of the Porsche and retrieved their luggage. Another man, lanky, and balding, exited the sedan. He and Burke exchanged a few words then the man who'd delivered the sedan, popped the trunk and removed a bicycle. As Eve got out of the Porsche, the man hopped on and rode away.

Eve wasn't wearing shoes and took careful steps over the gravel to the sedan. Burke turned to her. "Your suitcase is on the back seat. Take a minute and put something on."

He walked away from the car and stood facing the road. Eve climbed onto the back seat. The previous occupant of the car had left the engine idling. The radio was tuned to a rhythm and blues station. At the moment, Aretha belted out "Natural Woman" to the accompaniment of the hum from the sedan's air conditioning system set to low.

Eve removed Burke's jacket and the towel beneath. They were in the middle of nowhere. Another car could drive up this dirt road and see her in the nude. She shook her head. Her modesty was certainly misplaced, given everything else she had to be concerned about. Still, she dressed quickly in underthings, a pair of linen walking shorts in a salmon color, and a matching blouse. A pair of sling-back sandals completed her outfit.

"Ready," she called out to Burke when she left

the car, though, at the slam of the door, marking her departure from the back seat, he'd already turned and begun to walk back to the car.

Burke got in the driver's side and Eve joined him up front.

He bent and looked under the steering column.

"What are you doing?" she asked.

"This car is equipped with a tracking device. I'm disabling it."

"You don't want anyone to be able to find us," she said softly.

"No."

Her thoughts started to spin. "Who don't you trust?" At his steady gaze, Eve pushed. "My life is on the line. I have a right to know what's going on."

"I'm just being cautious."

Eve wasn't buying that. "The bomb was the second attempt. I repeat, I did not make an error in my insulin injection last night. I know you don't believe me but someone switched the insulin in my pen injectors."

"I believe you." His gaze locked with hers before returning his attention to the drive. "I'd say the bomb was an attempt to correct the botched insulin attempt. I have to hand it to whoever did that. The plan was an excellent one. If you hadn't gotten help when you did, you would have slipped into a diabetic coma. By the time I went looking for you in the morning, you would have been dead."

A thin layer of sweat broke out on Eve's skin.

"We would have concluded as Malhi had,"

Burke went on, "that you'd simply made a mistake and taken the wrong insulin last night. Your death would have been ruled accidental. Though if that mattered to your assassin, it no longer does since he used a bomb this time."

Eve's throat tightened and she swallowed to clear it. "Apparently not."

"Your hair dryer must have been rigged while we were at the hospital." Burke's mouth tightened into a thin line that bespoke his anger.

"Who would want me dead? And who would have had the opportunity to switch the insulin? We need to find out who had access to my insulin since yesterday? The only people I've been in contact with since then have been the chemists at the conference, and you Burke." Eve arched her brows. "Have you decided to execute me?"

Burke gave her another level look. "We can start by asking your friend Alasdair McHampton."

"Allie?"

"He was in possession of your purse."

A fierce protectiveness for her friend surged through her. "Allie would never hurt me!"

"That remains to be seen."

"You can't think if Allie were the one who wanted me dead, he would be stupid enough to reveal that he had my purse? That makes no sense."

"We've already concluded that had you gone into a diabetic coma and died, it would have appeared an accident. McHampton had no reason to hide the fact that he had your purse."

Eve chewed her lower lip then said softly, "You can't harass him. He has a heart condition and the stress of being questioned might bring on an attack." Her voice softened further. "It can't be Allie."

Burke watched her for a time then surprised her by conceding.

"It maybe just a coincidence that McHampton happened to pick up your purse," Burke said. We need to look into that. But someone tipped our guy off, or knew that Patterson was dead and that I took his place." Burke eyed her. "Got any other ideas who that might be, Doctor?"

"You aren't going back to suggesting that I tipped Richard's buyer off because—"

Burke looked like that was exactly what he was thinking.

"You're unbelievable," she said. "Someone tried to kill me and you're blaming me."

"You could have let the buyer know about Richard Patterson so he wouldn't show up for the meeting. You weren't expecting him to turn on you. It's possible your buyer got nervous about you being discovered by law enforcement and wants you out of the way."

"And what about getting the formula from me?"

"He may think you pose enough of a threat that taking you out is worth forfeiting the formula. I don't know at this point."

"So you think Richard's buyer is the one who switched my insulin?"

"It wouldn't take long to make the switch. Could have been made at the conference when your purse was unattended. It's possible that he may be looking to cover his tracks completely and stymie the investigation by eliminating our one lead—you."

It seemed pointless to tell Burke again that she wasn't a lead to Richard's buyer. "By making my death appear accidental, he would not have exposed himself. But a bomb." Eve shook her head slowly. "As we already said, whoever this is, he isn't concerned about making my death look like an accident."

"We already connected you to Richard and this deal. No way to try to hide that link. Looks like the buyer's only concern now is breaking the link by taking you out."

Eve frowned as Burke made a change to the route they'd been driving. "I hate to point this out but Washington is in another direction."

"We're not going to Washington."

"Oh?"

"I'm taking you to a safe house."

"Why?"

Burke raised an eyebrow. "I would have thought you'd be glad."

"That's not the point. Why the change in plan?"

He glanced at her. "We need you to disappear for a short while. Since the meeting with the buyer didn't happen, and you're under suspicion of treason, our next step is for me to transport you to Washington for questioning. Your assassin would be expecting that and may take the opportunity to make another attempt on your life. I don't plan to give him that opportunity."

Eve released a shaky breath. "Good thinking. So, where are we going? The CIA must have places set up for this kind of thing."

"We're not going to an Agency house. I want a place that can't be linked to the agency."

"Where then?"

"I have just the place."

* * *

The "place" turned out to be Burke's own cabin deep in the woods of West Virginia. After driving for hours with only brief rest stops, and a quick dash into a convenience store for supplies, they arrived as the first streaks of dawn tinted the sky pink.

The cabin was well appointed with a generator that provided creature comforts like electricity for appliances and for heating water that was provided by a well.

"There's just the one bedroom," Burke said. "Go ahead and take it. I'll bunk on the couch."

Eve didn't protest his offer of the bedroom. She was so tired, she could have slept standing up. Still, inside, she glanced around and then over her shoulder at the closed front door. It was a frightening thing to know that someone wanted you dead. Until two days earlier, her biggest problem was how to satisfy the occasional difficult client.

Burke's gaze softened on her. "You're safe here." He spoke the words gently. "No one knows about this place. You could say it's my haven."

He shrugged, as if embarrassed to admit to the weakness of needing a refuge from what had to be a job where he met the worst of humanity and saw all manner of atrocities mankind could perpetuate on each other.

When she'd been on the police force, she'd been detached from the crimes and the victims. She didn't have a lot of field experience because her application to work in forensics had been accepted shortly after she joined the LAPD. She hadn't seen human suffering up close, but from the distance of a microscope.

Burke's admission of vulnerability softened her opinion of him a little, which was the last thing she wanted. He still didn't believe her claim of innocence. He was only protecting her now because it served his own purpose since she was his only lead to the buyer. His concern for her was professional. The bottom line: She was a job to him and a means to apprehending a criminal. She couldn't forget that she couldn't trust him and they were on opposite sides.

She went into the bathroom, opened her purse, and removed her pen injectors and the items needed to take her insulin. She opened each injector and matched the labels on the bottles to those on the injectors. Unlikely she'd ever skip that step again. Satisfied, she proceeded with the injection.

She was exhausted and needed sleep, but she was also now thirsty. She wouldn't be able to sleep until she'd had something to drink.

Instead of going to Burke's room, she padded out to the kitchen, careful not to disturb Burke, who might be asleep on the couch in the living area. He wasn't on the couch, but in the kitchen, making coffee. His jaw was darkened with stubble. He'd changed from a suit into jeans. He wasn't wearing a shirt, and all of her suspicions about what was beneath the conservative suit were confirmed. He had a hard, athletic body.

He glanced at her. "Want a cup?"

Eve nodded. "And a glass of water."

"Bottled water is in the fridge. Help yourself."

Eve did. The water wasn't cold since the generator that powered the fridge hadn't been on long enough to cool the fridge, but Eve took a long drink anyway.

The coffee maker hissed and sizzled. Burke pushed off the counter, took two mugs from the cupboard above the machine. "Milk?"

"Yes."

He took a carton of preserved milk from the pantry cupboard and opened it, then tilted the spout over her cup. Eve joined him at the counter and accepted the mug he held out to her.

He left his black.

Watching her he said, "You don't trust me any more than I trust you. But the stakes have changed for you now that Richard's buyer has tried to take you out."

Eve felt resentment rising, but held her tongue, letting him get it all out.

"We've now been placed in a position where we have the same objective, rather than before when finding the buyer for you would mean that he would implicate you and give us what we need to create an air tight case against you. Being in prison beats being dead. If you have anything you want to tell me about your relationship with the buyer, now's the time." Burke held her gaze.

Eve stared at him in stony silence.

"Okay," Burke said, after a moment, his voice tight. "Your call."

He turned away from her. His disbelief fueled her anger. She forced herself to move past it. She had a bigger more important matter to focus on.

"Whoever planted the bomb also tampered with my insulin injectors. That means that someone had to get close enough to me to make that switch." She pushed off the counter and paced the small kitchen space in quick steps, her urgency mounting. "We need to go over who I've had contact with since yesterday. Other than Allie," she said firmly. "Who else had access to my purse to switch my insulin? I left my purse unattended during Dr. Abernathy's lecture while you and I followed the instructions in the text message. Someone at that lecture could have gained access to my purse. We need to review the backgrounds on the chemists at the conference."

She noticed that Burke hadn't said a word and she stopped pacing to face him.

"Finished?" he asked.

"That'll do for a start."

"There is no start. At least not for us. Lanski is handling the investigative part."

She arched her brows. "Your people think I'm a traitor. Just how hard will they work to find my assassin?"

Burke leaned back against the counter. "They'll do their jobs, regardless of their personal distaste for the assignment. And if you choose not to believe that, we still want the buyer. Your assassin may lead us to the buyer. Our job, yours and mine, is to lay low and let my people do what they need to do."

Burke was right. Finding her assassin may lead to finding the buyer. She felt some measure of comfort, but still wanted to be active in the investigation. "Don't forget I was a cop. You can't expect me to just sit around here and do nothing while someone is out there planning on how to kill me."

"That's exactly what I expect and what you will do. I'd also rather be out hunting this guy myself than being your babysitter."

"Babysitter!"

"That's right. Tough break for us both, Doctor. Look upon the next couple of days as a reprieve."

He downed the last of the coffee in his mug, then set it in the sink. Eve watched him make his way to the burlap couch. She was certain her anger was palpable.

"A reprieve?" She strode to the couch. "I need to find out who tried to kill me. I need to clear my name."

Burke sat on one of the thick cushions and tilted his head back to look up at her. The angle showed his strong jaw, dark with stubble.

"For the next couple of days, you're going to stay put. Here. With me. We're both going to have to accept that. Now, I'm going to get some sleep. You slept like a well-fed baby last night in the hospital. I know because I watched you. Which means I didn't sleep at all. A sleepless night combined with ten hours of driving to get here has me a little tired. I'm going to shut down for a few hours. I suggest you do the same."

He lay down and released an audible and Eve believed an involuntary sigh. He'd been running on adrenaline and sheer force of will for thirty six hours. Eve felt a flutter of compassion which she tamped down. It was his fault she was in this mess in the first place. Well, Richard's actually, but if Burke believed her claim of innocence, then they would be working together to find the accomplice and then through the accomplice the buyer instead of being adversaries.

"Burke—"

"Oh, if you're thinking of running out and trying to track down the buyer yourself to cut a deal and maybe save your hide, I'd advise you to consider that you're in dense woods here, miles from a road, and there's a lake opposite us. I have keys to both the car and the boat docked out front in the pockets of these jeans I'm wearing. I sleep light. Don't think you can get the keys out without waking me. And, if you decide to stick your hands in my pockets, I just may think you're there for another reason altogether."

Eve gave him a fulminating look. "On top of being arrogant, you've got quite an ego. Must get heavy, carrying it around."

Burke closed his eyes. "Turn off the light on your way out, would you?"

Eve had more fight left in her, but Burke had dismissed her. An instant later, his breathing slowed and his chest rose in the deep even rhythm of sleep.

She had more to say to him, but it was going to have to wait. She turned out the light and went to Burke's room.

The room held only an armoire, nightstand, and a bed. The furniture was large, the bed massive. Eve stretched out on the mattress. The bed was made with sheets patterned with blue stripes. They smelled faintly of lemon and were fresh, and crisp. Burke must have made up the bed while she'd been in the bathroom, taking her insulin injection.

Either he liked a lot of space when he slept, or he didn't sleep alone when he was up here. The thought of Burke tangling in the sheets with a woman did strange things to her insides. She pushed the thought away.

She was angry at him over their argument and didn't think she'd be able to sleep, but fatigue outweighed the anger and she did sleep. She awoke to the smell of bacon frying. The bedroom faced east and caught the first morning rays but with the progression of the sun, the room was now in twilight. She glanced at her watch, squinting to make out the numbers in the dimness. One o'clock. Afternoon. She'd slept half the day away. She couldn't remember the last time she'd done that.

She'd slept in her clothes. Her shorts and blouse were wrinkled. She hadn't looked in a mirror, but she knew that her dark hair was wild upon awakening. She had no reason to think today would be the exception to that rule. Since she slept on her stomach, squashing her face into the pillow beneath her head, her eyes tended to be puffy and droopy when she rose from her slumber.

Normally, she would make herself presentable

before facing another person. She spotted her suitcase by the front door where Burke must have left it. She'd have to walk past him to get it. So much for making herself presentable before facing him.

She leaned back against the wall and bowed her head. With the state her life was in, her appearance was her least concern.

She padded over the worn wood floor to the kitchen, following the scent of coffee and the promise of caffeine. Burke stood at the stove, cracking eggs into a sizzling skillet. The eggs made a hissing sound as they struck the hot pan.

He wore jeans again but had added a shirt. His dark hair was damp from a recent shower and combed back from his face. He'd shaved exposing the hard jaw line that seemed to always draw her eye when she glanced at him. She looked away from it, from him.

His gaze lifted from the skillet at her approach and honed on her. His jaw tensed. In reaction to her rumpled state? Was he a man who expected women to be perfectly groomed all the time? Thinking that about him, she reluctantly admitted caused a sense of disappointment. For some reason, she'd expected better of him.

He was blocking her view of the coffee maker. "Is there coffee?"

Burke stepped aside, clearing a path and revealing a three-quarters full pot. The mug she'd used the night before was washed and draining on a rubber mat. She moved closer to him to retrieve the mug and fill it. His body tensed and he took another step away from her. Well, damn, she needed some tidying up, but his reaction was getting downright insulting.

Burke's own mug stood near the pot. He clasped it by the base rather than the ear, his large hand completely covering a decal of the Blue Ridge Mountains.

Eve went to the fridge and helped herself to the milk. Burke returned to the skillet.

The aroma wafting from the pan made Eve's mouth water. She'd had no more than a greasy burger from a twenty-four hour fast food drive thru the night before. Burke had eaten the same and as he went about filling two plates with eggs, bacon, potatoes, and toast with portions suitable for a team of lumberjacks, it was obvious that he was famished as well.

She gained further evidence of that when he dug in and cleared his plate before she'd had little more time than to settle onto the wooden kitchen chair.

* * *

Burke forced himself to keep his gaze on his plate—and not on the woman seated across from him at his table. It was turning out to be a monumental task. She was an attractive woman, no doubt about it, and she knew how to make the most of her looks. She had the makeup and fashion thing perfected to an art. Yeah, she was pretty, and he couldn't deny that beauty jump started his heart and his libido every time he saw her, but seeing her in his kitchen a few moments ago had nearly induced a coronary.

Here she was, straight from bed—his bed—her long, dark hair wild around her face and spilling to her shoulders. Her eyes heavy-lidded from sleep. And her scent—there was a scent coming off her that didn't come from a cosmetics bottle. It was pure woman and unique to her. The wild hair, pouty lips ... and that scent. He wanted nothing more than to take her back to his bed and make love with her until they both were too exhausted to move. And then, he wanted to make love with her all over again.

Of course that was out of the question. Of all the women in the world, why did he have to want this one? He'd known attractive women before. Truth be told, women who were more beautiful than Eve. But, they hadn't made him want the way she did.

He felt a measure of disgust with himself for having any thoughts about her that weren't professional. She was suspected of treason. She had created a weapon to kill innocent people for her own profit. If she hadn't been found out, and by people who put their lives on the line every day to save lives—including her own—her plot would have been successful.

That thought grated. Her betrayal of her own people grated. His gaze lifted to hers involuntarily, however and his body reacted again.

"I cooked," Burke said. "You clean up."

He pushed his chair back from the table, got to his feet and left the cabin.

CHAPTER EIGHT

Eve watched him go. Clearly, he was angry. But about what? She felt her own temper spark. She'd had every intention of cleaning up after the meal. But if he thought he could take advantage of their situation and issue an order for kitchen duty, he could think again.

She finished the meal, which was excellent, washed her own plate and mug and set them on the drainer. She needed her insulin, a shower and then she'd feel better.

A few moments later, Eve stepped under the hot spray. Leaning against the shower stall, she stood unmoving, letting the water sluice down her skin and ease the tension from her body. She tried to clear her mind of the last forty eight hours. Was that all it had been? Since Richard's death. Since she'd learned she was suspected of terrorism. Since two attempts had been made on her own life. So much had happened and in such a short time. She prayed that the next forty eight hours would see this mess resolved and her life restored.

When she entered the living and dining room area, she saw that Burke hadn't come back inside. She was alone.

She rubbed her temples where a headache was building. Burke wanted her to sit idle and let the CIA find out who was behind the attempts on her life. She could not believe that her assassin was Allie. Who then? It went against her nature to sit back and wait for Burke's associates to find the one trying to kill her. But just what was she going to do and from here?

Burke's laptop was on the coffee table. Normally, she'd ask his permission to use his computer, but she ignored what she would normally do—this was hardly a normal situation—and went to the couch.

The blanket, pillow, and sheet he'd used were heaped against one arm of the sofa. Eve sat on the center cushion and booted up the laptop. It was likely that Burke had the system password protected, but she had to try to get in.

She needed a list of the conference attendees. It was a logical place to start to try to find the person who'd switched her insulin. Burke may have all of that on his system. She and Richard had registered for the conference weeks ago and it was likely that Burke would have a record of that. He would have compiled a list of the chemists attending all of the lectures and events she and Richard were scheduled to attend. If she'd been working this case, she would have gathered that information. Someone attending the Abernathy lecture could be the accomplice and the accomplice could be the one who accessed her purse and switched her insulin.

As she'd suspected, Burke's system was password protected. She was no hacker and had only a rudimentary knowledge of how computers worked. What would Burke use as a password? She knew nothing about the man that would provide a clue. Not even his birthday. She was finished before she'd started. There was no help for it. She was just going to have to ask him.

She was about push off the couch and go in search of him when Burke entered the cabin. Their gazes locked. He didn't look particularly angry at finding her at his laptop. In fact, he would have walked right by her, out of the common living space, but she spoke.

"I need access to your system. I need a list of the chemists who attended the Abernathy lecture with us. That person may be the one behind the attempts on my life."

"We've been through this. You don't need to do anything at the moment except lay low."

"This is my life. My freedom. No one cares as much about it as I do. No one will fight as hard as I will." When Burke didn't respond, she added. "Okay, then, I want to go to Washington. If you're not going to do anything to find the guilty party now, I don't need to be here. I want to hire a lawyer and a private investigator to work on my case. We're just wasting time here. The longer we wait, the colder the trail will get."

"Have you forgotten that your life is in danger?"

A tremor went through her but she fixed him with a steely look. "I'll take that chance."

"The choice isn't yours to make. It's mine and we're staying here."

Eve didn't respond to Burke's comment, seeing no point in it. His mind was made up.

Since he made no move to reclaim his laptop, Eve returned to the task of trying to figure out Burke's password.

* * *

Burke watched Eve bend over his laptop again. Shoulders hunched slightly, she gently tapped the keyboard. Her features were a study in concentration with her brows drawn together and her soft brown eyes fixed on her task.

There was no way she was going to be able to figure out his password. She'd soon grow tired of the task. As for himself, he needed to call Lanski.

Burke left the cabin. A bird chirped from somewhere nearby. It was a warm day. He rubbed the back of his neck that was knotted with tension and damp from perspiration. The lake beckoned. He cast a longing glance at it, then resigned to playing babysitter, pulled out his phone from the back pocket of his jeans.

Lanski did not pick up so Burke left a message, including that it wasn't urgent. He was seeking an update on Alasdair McHampton. Burke closed the phone with a loud snap. He felt tense, edgy, at loose ends. He wasn't used to being on the fringes of an investigation and sitting idle. Being at the cabin didn't help. Usually when he was here, he made the most of the slow pace, so unlike what he was accustomed to on the job. He took time to recharge after being drained from an assignment. Part of the problem was that his haven had been breached on this trip. It was not his haven this visit. This trip it was a safe house. He'd brought his work with him. He frowned. And who was he kidding? His problem wasn't that he'd brought his work to the cabin, but that his work was Dr. Eve Collins.

He shouldn't have brought her here. Hell, he shouldn't be the one to guard her. He should have assigned another agent to that task once he realized how fiercely attracted to her he was.

He'd been a poor guard. While on his watch, there'd been two attempts on her life. Was that because in his attempt to put distance between himself and Eve, he'd been careless, overlooked something? He couldn't deny the possibility. He was never careless on an assignment. Yet he'd never had an assignment like this one where he'd found his suspect distracting.

Burke recalled again how she'd almost died from the insulin switch. Her corpse-pale face as paramedics had rushed her to an ambulance. He rubbed a hand down his face at the memory. His hand came away wet with fresh perspiration.

And then there'd been the bomb. He went still, recalling it.

Both attempts occurred while in his care. While under his protection. There would not be a third attempt. He gritted his teeth. He'd make sure of that. He would keep her safe. He would keep her safe until he could deliver her to

Washington, he added.

The telephone he was still holding remained silent. Willing it to ring wouldn't make it do so. He rolled his taut shoulders. He needed to do something other than wait for the phone to ring. Other than think about the woman sleeping in his cabin, in his bed.

The grass on his land had grown several inches since he'd last been here and there was a leak in one of the windows that he wanted to fix. Might as well do what he could to spend the frustration and use this time on his hands to do some routine maintenance on the cabin. He headed for the shed.

Two hours later, satisfied with his progress, Burke returned to the cabin. He was parched and he needed a shower. His shirt was matted to his back with perspiration. He rubbed the back of his neck. By now Eve would have given up trying to determine his password and moved onto something else. He had to hand it to her though, she was putting on quite a show of innocence. But then, faced with the prison terms she was looking at, she would grasp at any straw to try to get herself out of the charges she faced.

Prison term ... the thought of Eve in prison for her crime should have brought on the usual satisfaction he felt when apprehending a criminal. It didn't.

Burke opened the door to the cabin with more force than was necessary. He wanted a gallon of water and headed to the fridge. He stopped short. Eve was in the same position she'd been in when he went outside, hunched over his computer.

She didn't glance up from the screen at his entrance.

"What are you doing?" he asked.

She looked up then, gave him a brief but steady look before returning her gaze to the screen without uttering a word.

She was still trying to break his password. Despite his efforts, Burke felt a grudging admiration for her tenacity.

"There isn't anything on my hard drive about your case," he said. "Gaining access to my files won't do you any good. Remember my laptop was here at the cabin when we arrived. I didn't bring it with me. I haven't used it to work your case."

She gave him that steady look again, her beautiful eyes unflinching.

"Maybe not," she said. "But you could use it to connect to your agency's data base. From there we could get the list of chemists who attended Abernathy's lecture and do background checks on them. One of them is the buyer or an assassin working for the buyer."

"All of that is being done."

"By your people, I know," Eve muttered.

Her gaze lowered, but before it had, he'd seen dejection in her eyes. Seeing her dejected bothered him. He didn't like that it did. She needed something to sustain her, something to occupy her time so she didn't feel useless and out of control. It was not his responsibility to entertain her or to boost her morale, but seeing her dejected when she'd shown such courage so far bothered him. He supposed it wouldn't hurt to indulge her in this.

Burke took two bottles of water from the fridge then joined her on the couch. His blanket and pillow were neatly folded on one of the faded arms of the old sofa. She had positioned herself on the middle cushion, leaving him just enough room to fit between her and the arm that held the bedding. When he sat, his legs brushed hers. She wore jeans so her legs were covered, but the contact sparked the memory of the long, lithe legs he'd glimpsed following the bombing, when she'd been wearing nothing but a towel and then after that only his suit jacket.

With a monumental effort, he banished that memory and typed in his access code. He felt her gaze on him, trying to decipher his quick key strokes. He decided to give it to her. He'd just change the code later.

"Magdalena," he said.

"What?"

"My password is Magdalena."

Her brow furrowed. "Oh. That's unusual. An old girlfriend or," she hesitated, "your wife's name?"

He narrowed his gaze on the computer screen as he went on entering codes that would link him to the agency's computers. "Nothing so dramatic. And I'm not married. Magdalena was the name of a stray dog my family took in when I was a kid."

"Oh."

The surprise in her voice had him glancing up at her. "What? You figured I don't like dogs or that I was hatched?"

She met his gaze. Humor glinted in her eyes

now as she shrugged. “Maybe both.”

Burke laughed. She laughed too. For an instant he was captivated by her mouth. He looked away from it and returned his attention to his computer.

“We looked at all the chemists.”

Eve slid forward on the cushion. “And?”

“Nada.”

“There has to be someone.” Eve’s expression reflected her disappointment but she straightened her posture. “Who is on the list?”

He was now linked to the agency files on her case. He brought up the list of chemists who’d registered for Abernathy’s lecture.

“One-hundred-nine, including Richard Patterson and you,” Burke said.

“That many.” Eve nodded. “Then I’d better get started.”

* * *

Three hours later, they had researched all of the registrants. Eve hadn’t expected Burke to help her, but he remained with her. Nothing leaped off the screen screaming terrorist. Eve’s shoulders slumped slightly in disappointment. Really, though, what had she expected?

She now knew more about Allie and the other chemists than she wanted to and didn’t know how she would face them again now that she’d invaded their privacy and learned personal things about them she had no business knowing. And all for nothing. She was no closer to finding out who’d switched her insulin than when she’d started.

"Ugh!" She flung herself back against the cushions of the sofa.

Burke eyed her. "You'd be hell on a stake out."

"I never went on stake outs. My work was confined to the forensics lab, which I'm sure you know. I was hoping that my personal acquaintance with some of the chemists might give me an edge your people don't have. That something about one of them might strike me as out of place."

"You gave it a shot. We need a break."

"No. No. We need to continue. We need—"

"A break." Burke insisted. "It's dinner time. I'm starving and you must be too." He got to his feet, stretched then yawned. "Come on let's see what we can put together."

The wary look Eve gave him provoked a laugh out of him. "Don't look so skeptical. I'm not the greatest cook, but I proved earlier that I can put a meal together. If you aren't too fussy," he added.

Eve got to her feet as well. The dishes from their breakfast, the breakfast he prepared, still sat on the kitchen table. She felt petty about not having cleaned up earlier and now began stacking plates then carrying them to the sink. While she washed, Burke went to a pantry cupboard beside the fridge. He withdrew a can of tomato sauce and a wrapped package of spaghetti.

He held up his fare. "It's plain but you won't starve."

Eve finished washing the last plate then placed it in the dish drainer on the counter. "Doesn't have to be plain."

"'Fraid so. I keep only canned and dry goods here. No fresh spices and since we're laying low, I'd rather not leave here to get any."

Eve dried her hands on a checkered dish towel. "No need to go anywhere. Not a grocery store anyway. We have more than we'll need right outside."

At Burke's frown, Eve smiled. "Come with me."

"Said the spider to the fly," Burke murmured.

Eve laughed. "Where do you keep your bowls?"

"Bottom right cupboard."

Eve withdrew a large stainless steel mixing bowl then led the way to the door. Outside, Burke fell into step beside her. She breathed deeply of the fresh air. If not for her situation, she would have enjoyed being at the cabin. She liked the earthy and animal smells. She liked being surrounded by the beauty of trees and wildlife that far outshone anything man could make in the city.

Eve followed a path into the trees. Sunlight poked through the branches and dappled the ground on which they walked. She set a slow pace, meandering around various patches of plant growth, bending over glorious outcroppings of lush green leaves and stems. She came to a mushroom patch and stopped.

"Those are great in sauces." She pointed to the patch.

Burke shook his head slowly. "Not a good idea. Haven't you heard? Mushrooms can be lethal."

"Certainly, but not those. I often blend herbs

and spices to make the scents I use in cosmetics, so I know which are poisonous and which aren't. Those," she pointed again, "aren't."

He still looked doubtful and she laughed. "Don't worry. I know what I'm doing."

She stooped before the mushroom patch that covered several feet of ground and examined the crop. She plucked several plump specimens and placed them in the bowl. She shot to her feet. "Next."

"Next?"

"Let's see what else we can find." She walked on, leaving Burke to follow. When he fell into step beside her again she looked up at him. "How long have you been coming here?"

"I bought the place about ten years ago."

"Are you from West Virginia?"

"Chicago."

"So tell me, since you weren't hatched and like dogs, do you have family?"

He smiled. "Parents. Younger sister. Older brother. My brother has a big, noisy family."

Big, noisy family. She felt a pang. Once she'd hoped to have a big, noisy family of her own.

"You okay?" Burke asked.

She'd come to a stop. Eve put the wistful thought from her mind. "I'm fine."

She dropped the subject of family and focused on her reason for being in these woods. She spotted a circle of wild chives and bent over them. Perfect. She added several to the bowl. A few steps away, dandelions sprouted. She picked a handful of them as well.

At Burke's arched eyebrow, Eve grinned. "Boil

dandelion stems and they taste like spinach."

"Hard to believe."

"You'll be eating those words. Literally. We have enough. We can head back."

Back at Burke's cabin, Eve filled a pot with water then set it on the stove to boil. She took the skillet she'd washed from the drainer, poured a dollop of oil into the pan, then set it on the stove as well. She dumped the contents of the bowl she'd filled from the forest into the sink and treated her pickings to a thorough cleansing. That done, she chopped the vegetables and plopped them into the skillet.

The aroma of sautéing vegetables and rich tomato sauce filled the air. Eve transferred the contents of the skillet, now gently browned, to the bubbling sauce and lowered the heat. The water reached boiling point and she unwrapped the pasta and placed it in the pot.

Fifteen minutes later, Eve turned to Burke. With a flourish, she said, "Dinner is served."

She drained the dandelions she'd boiled, added salt and pepper and offered the bowl to Burke. From her place across the table from him, Eve watched him taste a stem.

His brows arched and his wary expression became one of surprise. "I'll never look at dandelions in the same way again."

Eve smiled. "Told 'ya."

Burke forked up a portion of sauce and vegetable coated pasta. "Where did you learn to cook like this?"

The smile left Eve's face. She lowered her gaze to her plate. "My daughter Emily had several food allergies. I consulted an herbalist on how to make her meals more palatable using spices and herbs that she didn't react to. We didn't live near a wooded area and some things were unavailable in grocery or health food stores, so Em and I started a garden in our yard and grew only the things that she could eat. She loved to discover new things we could plant there."

Eve felt Burke's gaze on her, but couldn't meet his eyes yet. She rose to her feet, seized her plate and the now empty bowl of dandelion greens from the table and dashed to the sink.

Burke's chair scraped across the wood floor. He came up behind her and placed his hand on hers, now immersed in soapy water.

"I know that your daughter was killed in a car accident five years ago. I'm sorry," he said softly, linking their fingers beneath the suds.

Five years had not dulled the pain of Emily's death. Tears burned her eyes. She wanted to be alone when they fell.

"It's been a long day." The words tumbled out of Eve's mouth in her urgency to flee. "I'll do the dishes in the morning. Good night."

* * *

He felt a surge of anger and took another turn around the hotel room he'd been staying in since the start of the chemist's conference. His cover had served him well, providing him with the opportunity he needed to remain close to his prey.

Until recently. His prey had eluded him.

He clenched his fists. Where were they? All of his efforts so far had failed to turn up where Eve Collins and Burke had gone to ground.

Eve Collins was proving to have as many lives as a cat. She'd cheated death—twice. His attempts to kill her had failed. The last attempt that should have gotten the job done had, instead, put Eve and Burke on alert. Sent them into hiding. He swung around and slammed his fist into the nearest wall.

His efforts had also failed to turn up the formula.

Time was running out. The people he worked for were getting anxious for their product. He swallowed and broke out in a sweat. It wouldn't do to keep these people waiting.

He took a calming breath. It was time to finish this—to get the formula and to get rid of the loose end that was Eve Collins—and he knew just how to do it.

CHAPTER NINE

Burke knocked on his bedroom door. An image of Eve, sprawled across his bed, her glorious hair wild as it had been yesterday when she'd awakened, flashed in his mind and he broke into a sweat. He shook his head to clear it, then knocked again, louder.

"Eve, wake up."

His tone came out sharper than he'd intended. Hurried footsteps thudded across the wood floor then the door was flung open.

"What's happened?"

Her taut expression reflected her alarm. He shook his head and smiled to reassure her.

"Nothing. Yet. Get dressed, we're going out."

"Burke, it's five o'clock in the morning. We're in the middle of nowhere. Where do you suggest we go?"

She had one hand on her head, clutching the wild mane of hair. The impact to his senses was diffused but only slightly. Burke could feel himself reacting to her again and forced his thoughts back to why he was at her door.

"Fishing."

"What?"

"It'll be light in an hour. I warn you, it's cold on the lake at this time of the morning. Dress warm."

Eve blew a breath at a hunk of hair that lay across her eyes then turned away from Burke. "The only place I'm going is back to bed." Feet dragging, she followed up her words with action.

Burke trailed Eve back into his bedroom, and yanked a pair of sweat pants, a sweat shirt with a logo for the Chicago Bears and a pair of thick socks out of the armoire. "Put these on. I doubt you have anything warm enough in your bag."

He left without a backward glance to check, closing the door behind him. She hadn't balked at the invitation. It occurred to him that she might. Maybe she hadn't because she needed a distraction from the worry and fear of her situation.

He had to be out of his mind to suggest this. The last thing he needed was to spend more time in her company when the sight of her had his insides tightening.

To further torment him, an image of her standing as she had just been, fresh from his bed came to him. But on the heels of it came another image: Eve's face, ravaged, as she spoke of her daughter's death. Five years later, her hurt was still raw. Her pain had stayed with him long after she'd fled the kitchen to find what solace she could on her own.

He blew out a breath. Inviting her company was a mistake—a mistake he hadn't been able to stop himself from making.

He filled a thermos with coffee and she still hadn't emerged from his bedroom. Had he been wrong and she wasn't coming? He returned to the bedroom.

Two swift taps against the door then Burke called out, "The fish are waiting. You ready?"

Eve opened the door. She was holding a three-inch high shoe. "You'll have to go without me. I didn't pack shoes suitable for this occasion."

Burke's gaze lingered on her, taking her in. She was wearing the clothes he'd tossed at her, after rolling the shirt sleeves and the pant legs back several times. She looked adorable in his oversized clothing and sexy as hell. As she neared, he caught the scent of the lemon laundry detergent and an underlying fragrance that he was coming to identify as uniquely Eve.

He looked away from her and went back to the armoire. "I have another pair of athletic shoes. We'll put a sock inside to shorten them and since you'll be sitting in the boat, and not walking, they should serve well enough."

Sure enough, they did. Burke added one of his jackets to her ensemble and twenty minutes later, Eve sat across from him in his small fishing boat while he motored across a lake as smooth as glass. A rim of pink tinged the sky in the east.

Burke dropped anchor then cut the engine. Without the roar, he became aware of the buzz of an insect nearby, the cry of gulls, and the gentle lapping of the water against the hull. He reached into a tackle box that held tiny trays with lures and pulled out a black one. He spun the silver tail and caught the light. He pulled out a second lure that was lime green and held up both for Eve's inspection.

"Which would you like? Now I warn you, each has its merits and will attract different kinds of fish. For example, this lake is noted for its Bass, Walleye and Catfish. Some Bass fishermen will tell you that Bass like bright colors, like this orange." He raised the lure as he spoke. "The Walleye, on the other hand, sees most colors as either red or green so won't be influenced at all by color but goes for sparkle. Under the water, this silver tail glitters like a mirror. Another factor to consider when making your selection is daylight and water depth. Both will alter the activity of the fish and the appearance of the lure. Walleye are more active in dim light."

Eve's lips twitched. "I can see you've made a thorough study."

"Absolutely, I'm a thorough man."

He gave her a bland look and was rewarded when Eve's smile broadened.

"I have no doubt." She was fighting laughter. "But, I'd rather choose my own lure."

Her smile prompted one from Burke.

"Go for it." His smile widened to a grin.

She leaned over the box, examining the contents. "I'll take that gold one." She pointed to her choice.

Burke attached the lure to one of the two rods leaning against the side of the boat then got to his feet. When Eve did the same he moved to stand behind her and positioned her hands on the rod. He kept his hold loose, kept a foot of distance between their bodies to curb his reaction to her nearness. Fat chance. He raised her arms slowly, tossed back the fishing rod over her shoulder and sent out a cast that glided across the air, before softly plopping into the water.

Burke gave a satisfied sigh. He released Eve and prepared his own rod.

"How did you come across this place?" she asked.

"When I was a kid, my family used to come here for a week every summer, camping and fishing. The place stuck in my mind and one day I just said what the hell and bought a place for myself."

"You said you have an older brother and a younger sister?"

"Yeah."

"Makes it nice at holiday time."

He didn't miss the wistful note in her voice. "I don't always make it to holidays, but yeah, it's nice when I do."

"They back in Chicago? Home of the Bears."

Burke's gaze sharpened. "You a fan?"

Eve grinned. "No, but I also have brothers and they are."

"Actually, my brother and his family are there. My sister, Mallory, is a federal agent. She's assigned to the New York Bureau office."

"You and she must talk a lot of shop when you get together."

He could have shrugged off the statement and left it at that, didn't know why he added. "Some shop talk. I haven't heard from her in a while. With my work and her work, we don't keep in touch as much as we'd like." He'd give her a call as soon as this assignment was over and he was back at Langley.

"Any chance of getting a cup of that coffee?" Eve asked.

Burke leaned his rod against the ledge of the boat and uncapped a thermos. Steam rose into the air along with the aroma of coffee. He poured into two mugs and held one out to her which she accepted with an enthusiastic thanks.

Burke couldn't resist teasing her. He gave her a sideways glance. "Got any eye of newt we can add to the coffee?"

Eve laughed.

They sipped then fished in a companionable silence. She wasn't chatty on the lake. Burke appreciated that. He enjoyed the quiet and stillness of the water. The sun rose higher. The lake looked a clear blue. Eve finished her coffee, shook her head at a refill then took a seat, leaning against the padded back. The boat rocked gently with the current. She took a deep audible breath. Her eyes drifted closed. Burke watched her. He was watching her so closely, at first he didn't see the tip of her rod take a dip.

"Eve?" His tone was soft.

"Mmm."

"You have a bite."

Her eyes flew open. "Oh!"

* * *

Burke stood against the door of the cabin, gazing out at the moonlit night. Eve moved to stand beside him. Moonlight filtered through the leaves of the trees that rose above the cabin, dappling the earth with light. Crickets chirped nearby.

"Do you get out here much," Eve asked.

"Not as much as I'd like."

Eve took a deep breath of the crisp night air. "I can certainly understand your fondness for this place."

Burke turned to her, a smile tugging at his lips.

"You look surprised."

He gestured to her silk blouse and heels. "I didn't take you for being much for the great outdoors."

Acknowledging his point, Eve returned his smile. "Remember I mentioned that I have brothers? I have four of them. Vacations in the great outdoors were a regular thing in my house."

She hadn't planned on saying more on the subject, but Burke appeared intrigued.

She shrugged. "One year, I think I was about nine, my dad planned a camping trip with the boys. It was supposed to be some adventure—a man thing—my oldest brother told me. There was just enough of a challenge in his voice that there was no way I was going to be excluded from the trip. I went to my dad," her voice softened with the memory, "and asked him to take me along. He'd not meant to exclude me, he said, which I knew was the truth. He'd just presumed that I wouldn't be interested. Frankly, he was thrilled that I wanted to go along. My brothers put up a fuss, of course, but Dad would not have left me behind if I wanted to go along.

"That trip was four days in a bush with no amenities. Dad planned fishing and a nature hike and so our scent would blend with our natural surroundings, we didn't bathe in that time." Eve rolled her eyes. "We were pretty ripe by the end of it."

Burke smiled and leaned toward her. He sniffed audibly. "You smell wonderful."

Eve's smile spread. "This scent is one of my blends. I have to admit it's one of my favorites."

"It's great."

"We also develop men's aftershave."

Burke laughed. A rich sound she'd not heard from him. "I'll have to check that out."

"Burke ... it was nice ... today. Thank you."

"Day's not over. It's a beautiful night for a swim. How about it?"

"Why not?"

* * *

She'd packed a modest one piece swimsuit, intending to spend some time at the hotel's pool in between the events she'd registered for at the conference. She slipped into it and returned to the living room. When Burke emerged from the bathroom, clad only in black swim trunks, Eve was treated to the view of his magnificent body. Broad shoulders. Clearly defined abdominal muscles. Long, hard muscled legs. It had been a long time since Eve had taken inventory of a man's body. Somewhere in the last five years, since Emily's death, and the end of her marriage, Eve had lost interest in men. Interest in sex.

She averted her gaze from Burke. In one hand he carried his cell phone. With the other hand, he held the door open for her to precede him and they walked out into the night. Moon light silvered the water that lapped softly against a floating dock anchored to a post and the aluminum hull of Burke's fishing boat.

Burke stepped onto the dock. It pitched and swayed with his weight. He reached back and held out his hand for her. Eve placed her hand in his for an instant as she stepped onto the dock then, gaining her balance, hastily withdrew it. If Burke noticed her abrupt end to the contact with him, he said nothing.

She walked to the edge of the dock and lowered her foot into the water. She hastily withdrew it. In comparison to the warm, balmy air, the water felt ice cold.

"That's not the way to do it." Burke placed his cell phone on the dock then smiled like a shark. "This is the way."

He scooped her into his arms. Eve knew what was coming. She shrieked and grabbed his neck. Burke laughed and stepped off the dock with her in his arms.

She came up sputtering, arms flailing. But Burke hadn't left her once they'd gone under water. One arm had remained around her waist, was still around her waist, as he emerged, bringing her to the surface with him.

"I'm okay," she said.

He released her and she treaded water. "It's

nice once you're in."

Burke's grin gleamed in the moonlight. "Told 'ya."

Eve laughed as he repeated the phrase she'd spoken to him about the dandelions.

Burke dove below the surface. As Eve watched the water ripple gently in his wake, she thought, he was right: It was a beautiful night for a swim and just what she needed to ease some of the tension twisting her into knots.

Somewhere on land crickets chirped. She found the sound rhythmic and oddly soothing.

Burke broke the surface, coming up beside her. She felt in the mood to stretch her legs. In the distance, a trio of buoys, tied to a rope, bobbed in the water.

"Race you to the buoys and back," she said. She could feel the wide smile on her face. "Be warned, though, I competed in college." She wiggled her brows. "And I always won."

"A challenge. Say when."

Eve's grin widened. "When!"

She executed a perfect leap then dive that gained her several lengths as years of training reasserted themselves. Even allowing for the slight current that was present in the lake and not in a pool, Eve ate up the distance, stretching her legs and widening her stroke, easily finding her stride. Burke wasn't by her side. She slowed, taking a moment to glance up at the stars. She never saw the stars from her townhouse in L.A. City lights dulled the night. Here, the view was breathtaking.

She was caught up in the view when Burke

streaked by her. He'd moved like an eel, barely disturbing the water. Eve felt a smile spread across her face again and dove after him.

She put her all into the swim. She reached him and then with a smug glance he couldn't miss, passed him. At the buoys, she turned around. Burke was a mere half-length behind her now. She was laughing and she had to admit, panting, when she reached the dock an instant before he did. She looped one arm around a low rail on the dock, allowing the structure to keep her afloat. Burke pushed sopping hair back from his face then positioned himself in front of her and did the same.

He grinned. "You're good."

Eve nodded. "You should have seen me when I was competing."

Burke's gaze fixed on her. "You must have been quite a sight," he said softly.

Eve's heart, just now slowing to its normal rhythm, thumped. She focused on Burke. His eyes had darkened and his gaze was now intent on her. He raised his arm slowly from his side and brought it to her cheek. His gaze still on hers, he caressed her skin with his thumb.

Eve's breath caught. This was Burke. The man who believed her a traitor. She should pull back. Instead, when his lips parted slightly and he moved toward her, Eve moved to him.

His breath mingled with her own as their lips touched in a light, soft, caress, then Burke murmured something unintelligible, his hand lowered from her cheek to her waist and he brought her flush against him. She connected with his hard muscled body. A thrill coursed through her and she dug her fingers into his shoulder. Burke deepened the kiss, slanting his mouth across hers, opening his mouth. When his tongue slid between her parted lips, Eve met it with her own.

Her heart was racing now well beyond what it had been during the swim. Each breath came shallow and audible. She was quivering. Pressed against Burke, she felt every gasping breath he took and she felt the proof of his rampant desire pulse against her.

Something rang. Then again. Eve blinked then realized the ringing was from Burke's cell phone. He'd set it down on the dock, she recalled.

Burke's mouth left hers. He looked up through the wooden slats to the dock above them then drew back, releasing her. He was breathing hard. The tendons in his arms were taut. He shook his head as if to clear it, then rubbed a hand down his face. He reached up, grabbed the edge of one wooden plank and vaulted onto the dock.

Eve swam away from the rail she'd been holding. For some reason, the water now felt ice cold. Goose bumps pebbled her flesh.

She swam slowly, taking time to shake off what had almost happened with Burke. She'd literally been saved by the bell. Catastrophe averted. But where was the relief that should accompany that thought? She closed her eyes. It wasn't relief she was feeling.

By the time she reached Burke, he was closing his cell phone. Eve seized the dock as he had and hoisted herself up. Burke crouched, grasped her at the waist, and lifted her up beside him. Then he stepped away from her. The night air was chill. She picked up the towel she'd hung over the railing and draped it around her shoulders like a shawl.

"That was Lanski," Burke said. "Did Richard Patterson ever mention meeting Alasdair McHampton?"

Burke was all business again. "No, though Richard wouldn't have," Eve said. "He didn't know of my friendship with Allie. We didn't speak of personal things. But of course they weren't acquainted, Allie would have mentioned it."

"Would he?"

"Of course. And he certainly would have greeted you differently at the conference when I introduced you as Richard."

"My people learned that both Richard Patterson and Alasdair McHampton attended a small suburban chemist's conference several years ago. When Lanski asked him about Patterson, McHampton said he never knew a Richard Patterson until Dr. Collins introduced him to her business partner."

"If that's what Allie said, then that's it."

"The fact that Patterson and McHampton were both at that conference bothers me.

But, at this point, we have nothing more to link the two, so, yeah, as it stands now, that's it."

Eve nodded.

"Lanski is asking McHampton if he saw anyone handle your purse."

Eve didn't hold out any hope that Allie had. If

he had seen anyone with her purse, he would have mentioned it to her.

"I'm heading back," Eve said. "See you in the morning."

* * *

Burke watched her go, watched the gentle sway of her shapely derriere in the swimsuit. A few moments earlier, he'd had his hands on that beautiful part of her anatomy. His hands tingled with the desire to touch her again.

He shook his head. Eve was a suspected traitor. She was in his charge. Again, he asked himself: What was the matter with him?

She was attractive, yes, but he'd been attracted to other women many times, and hadn't been eaten up by the attraction.

That's what was happening to him. He was consumed by his attraction to Eve. He wanted to take her to bed so badly he couldn't think of anything else. He'd never had it this bad for any other woman.

Consumed by his attraction. But it was more than that. His attraction was more than sexual. He admired her courage that she'd displayed in this situation. He didn't know many others who would have taken death threats, and an accusation of treason with the fighting attitude she'd shown. She was a fighter, all right. From what he'd read in her file, she'd needed to be, given what she'd been through in the last years. Dismissal from the LAPD. The end of her six-year marriage. He'd read the profile on her. His fact sheets, though, summarized those events. They hadn't revealed the devastating impact they must have had on her life.

Those events took place on the heels of the death of her daughter. Eve was so hurt. The thought of her in pain unsettled him. He didn't like the fact that it did.

She'd gotten under his skin.

He had to get her out.

He rolled his shoulders to ease the tension there. A few more days and this would all be over. She would be out of his life. He would get back to his. The thought should have satisfied him. It didn't.

* * *

A cool breeze blew in through Eve's bedroom window, fluttering the gauze curtains. She was in bed but couldn't sleep. Small wonder. She was so churned up about Burke. He'd commented on her scent but his own—soap mixed with his own male smell—had intoxicated her.

He hadn't shaved that day and the dark stubble on his cheeks and chin made him look sexy. When he'd taken her in his arms she'd been up close to his tough, hard body, and felt each discreet muscle.

And she'd seen blatant desire in his eyes.

She wanted him, too. The admission stunned her. She hadn't been with a man since her marriage ended. Casual sex was available, should she have wanted it. She thought of Matt Deligne. She hadn't wanted it, though. She'd told herself that casual sex wasn't for her, and with Matt or any other man of her acquaintance that's all there would be. She told herself she was a relationship person. The desire to get to know a man well enough to want to go to bed with him had just never been there. But here and now, alone, in the dark and the quiet, she admitted the truth: She had simply stopped wanting sex. Her desire for sex had been gone for five years.

It was there now. In spades. With Burke.

It would have been handy to tell herself that after a five-year abstinence her body's natural sexual urge had reasserted itself. But she knew that wasn't the case. What she was feeling didn't stem from him as a man, but as *the* man.

He'd awakened feelings in her she'd thought dead. She should be applauding. Had the situation not been what it was, she would have acted on the desire she was feeling.

But their circumstances were what they were. As attractive as she found him, he was intent on proving her a traitor. If that didn't tamp down her desire, nothing would.

She rolled over. The short nightie she'd changed into after the swim bunched around her waist and she adjusted it. Her pillow was warm. She turned it over then flopped onto her back. She was making so much noise in here could Burke hear her in the outer room? She couldn't hear him. He was probably sleeping.

A branch snapped outside the cabin, jolting Eve from her thoughts of Burke. She sprang out of the bed. She crept to the window and flattened herself against the wall. The scent of pine wafted in on the breeze. She peeked out through the break in the curtains. The trees and underbrush outside her window were distinct in the moonlight, and all there was to see at the moment. Of course, if someone was out there, he'd hardly be standing in the open for her to view. Particularly since he'd stepped on a twig and put himself at risk.

Burke said no one knew about this place. To his knowledge, anyway. Eve wouldn't dismiss the possibility that someone had followed her and Burke here. Maybe wanting another try at killing her. It was frightening to think that, but also exhilarating. So far, she and Burke hadn't been having any success in identifying the one who wanted her dead. They needed a lead. Another attempt on her life would give them that and she would be glad of it. Even if it meant facing a killer.

Eve ducked beneath the window and returned to the bed where she'd left the shoes she'd worn earlier. She slipped them on then, keeping close to the walls, tiptoed out of the bedroom and into the short hallway beyond. The thick blue curtains in the outer room were drawn, effectively blocking any outside light. A small lamp on the long counter that separated the kitchen section from the living room glowed, and provided enough light for Eve to see the shadows of the furniture and to make out the front door.

A large shadow was making its way to that door at the moment. The arm was extended above the tall silhouette's head. At the end of it, was the outline of a gun. Eve knew that silhouette: Burke. He must have felt her gaze—or maybe he just sensed another presence in the room with him—because he turned to her.

"Burke!" She hissed his name loud enough for him to identify her and not shoot.

But he'd recognized her as well, she realized. Had known she was behind him before he'd turned. His gun hand had not wavered.

Eve met him by the door. "I guess you heard it, too."

"Yeah. Stay here while I check it out."

"No. I'm going with you."

"Stay here."

Eve shook her head. "If someone's followed us, we need to make sure he doesn't get away. We need to flank him, cutting off his escape routes."

"He might not be seeking escape. The noise might have been deliberate. A means to flush us out so he could take a shot. Stay here."

"More likely flush you out," Eve said. "Take you out first, then come inside and finish me. It's unlikely he'll be expecting both of us. I was a cop, remember? I know what I'm doing."

Burke's jaw tightened. A muscle there flexed briefly. "Hold on a minute."

Eve stared after Burke as he disappeared into his room, currently being occupied by her. What was he doing? They didn't have time to waste, but he was back quickly. He held out a gun.

"Take it."

Eve lowered her eyes to the gun and then raised her gaze to him. The gesture of trust surprised her and touched her.

"Ready," Burke asked.

She nodded and closed her fingers around the

gun butt.

Burke opened the door. Eve recalled her training and without either of them uttering a word, they slipped into standard police practice. Burke went high, Eve low, as they checked out the immediate area. The soft moonlight gave off a faint glow that wasn't overly bright, but still, Eve felt exposed. Again, she took in the tall trees and wide bushes, but that was all. No one stood outside the door, or pressed against a thick tree trunk.

Her work with fragrance kept her keenly aware of the scents around her. The sharp tang of pine and earth, still damp from the rain of the night, hung in the air. She couldn't detect any other fragrance. No spicy deodorant or cologne that would indicate someone other than herself and Burke was in the vicinity.

The sound had come from beyond the bedroom window at the back of the cabin. Eve motioned with the gun that she would go right. Burke nodded and headed in the opposite direction.

Now that she was outside, her short nightshirt was a poor covering. Light reflected off the soft yellow cotton and off of her exposed thighs, making her all too visible. Her shoes sank in the soft ground. She treaded carefully, keeping her weight off the heels.

No help for her clothing now. She put the thought out of her mind and kept her back against the cabin to assure no one could come up behind her.

There was no sign of anyone other than

herself. Burke was doing the same from the opposite direction. Since he hadn't called out, she knew he hadn't spotted anyone either. The woods would provide great cover for someone looking to hide in them. If whoever snapped that branch had decided to escape into the trees, they wouldn't find him. Particularly at night.

Burke's suggestion that someone may have lured them out in the open replayed in her mind. Eve felt an itch above her heart at the thought of someone shooting her from within the trees.

She reached the end of the cabin's exterior wall and, gun arm extended, whirled around the corner. Burke was already there.

He glanced at her. "I think we found our intruder."

He pointed to a trail of garbage. Eve fell into step beside him as he followed the trail of chicken bones and scraps that had been their dinner that evening. A short distance away, in the trees, they came upon a raccoon foraging in the bag Burke had discarded their garbage in. The animal had dragged the bag to that point.

The creature raised its eyes, shiny as marbles to them, then ran.

"A raccoon." Burke shook his head and laughed. "I forgot not to leave garbage outside. It has been too long since I've been up here."

Eve laughed too. She hadn't told Burke that the last time she'd spent a night outside of a city had been that camping trip with her father and brothers. She hadn't considered their intruder *could* be a woodland animal.

They made their way back inside the cabin for

another bag. Eve returned Burke's spare gun to him then they headed back outside to clean up the mess and secure the trash in the trunk of the car.

Eve's shoes no longer clung. She looked at her feet. Her sassy sling backs were now stretched from water seepage and caked with mud. The shoes were ruined. At least if they'd caught her would-be assassin, the loss would have been worth it.

"Intriguing attire for an apprehension," Burke said.

She certainly must look a sight in the short nightie and high heels. Burke was smiling again, a small sexy smile that had her heart picking up its pace. Eve shook off that unwelcome thought. "Yeah, well, I didn't think I should take time to get another pair from my suitcase."

She gave the shoes a slow remorseful shake of her head then stepped out of them and preceded him into the cabin. She turned to say good night. He stood backlit by the moon, his lean, hard body outlined. She couldn't see his face now, but she felt the weight of his gaze.

He raised his arm. She watched it in silhouette slowly reach out to her. She could have stepped back, out of his reach. This was Burke. *Burke. He* was all wrong. *This* was all wrong. But she remained in place, breath held, anticipating his touch.

Gently, he sifted his fingers through her hair, and when he cupped the back of her head, Eve rose on tiptoe and met his kiss. He brushed his lips across hers softly. Eve's eyelids lowered at his caress.

"Burke," she whispered.

"John. Say it, Eve. Say my name."

"John," she said. "John."

His hold on her tightened and he covered her mouth with his. His kiss was hot and hungry. Eve wrapped her arms around his neck, pulling him closer and holding him to her.

He sucked in his breath then his arms banded around her. He lifted her off her feet and held her tight against himself. His heart was pounding now, a hard thump thump or maybe that was her own.

He broke the kiss and their gasping breaths became the dominant sound in the room. He walked with her in his arms to the burlap couch and set her down gently on the soft cushions. He stretched out beside her, then his mouth was on hers again, kissing, tasting. He couldn't seem to get enough of her which was exactly how she was feeling.

He tugged the hem of her nightie. She raised her arms. He took his mouth from hers only long enough to lift the garment over her head and toss it somewhere into the darkness. His tongue slid over hers, then went deep. Her need for him surged. She scrambled to undo the buttons on his shirt, wanting so badly to touch him.

As soon as his shirt was open, he hastily removed it. His chest and arms were all muscle. Rock-hard, she discovered as she eagerly ran her hands over him.

His hands did not remain idle. They slid down her sides, her hips and her legs, taking her panties down with them. They, too, ended up somewhere in the darkness then he resumed his exploration, igniting fires where he touched. She'd removed her bra for sleep and he brushed her bare breasts with his thumbs. Pleasure streaked through her. His mouth left hers and went to her breasts, licking and sucking, alternating between them and taking her to a new level of need.

His breath was coming shorter and more shallow. As his hands and mouth moved over her, with ever increasing urgency, there were instants when Eve couldn't breathe at all.

He shifted position so they were no longer touching. An instant later, when his lower body brushed hers again she felt only skin. His jeans and shorts were now gone.

His eyes on her were hot enough to burn. He lowered his head. Their mouths were so close she felt his lips move as he murmured her name. His body rose above hers. She'd never been more aware of the vast difference in their sizes, of how much larger he was, and it thrilled her. His erection pressed against her. Despite his obvious urgency, he prodded her gently, testing her readiness. She shivered in anticipation and arched against him to show him just how ready she was.

Her slight movement seemed to push him to the edge of his control. He swallowed audibly and his every muscle tensed.

Slowly, so slowly, he filled her. Her body stretched to accommodate him and she sucked in her breath at the wealth of sensation. He pulled back then went deep. She dug her nails into his shoulders and when he picked up the pace, moving hard and fast, her vision grayed.

She moved with him, matching him stroke for stroke. She felt his body still, then her own tightened. Her body shuddered as Burke's did, and they found their release.

* * *

They'd made love on the scratchy burlap couch. Something was currently digging into Eve's hip. She didn't have the strength to move. Since John was still a dead weight on her, she figured he was in the same condition. She smiled. If she hadn't needed to breathe, she would have gladly kept him there for a day or two or forever.

Forever.

The blissful haze that was the aftermath of their lovemaking receded. The reality of their situation returned to her. Eve closed her eyes tight. What had she done?

She opened her eyes and gave his shoulder a nudge that was more forceful than necessary, and certainly wouldn't undo the last moments. "Burke?"

A few moments earlier he'd been "John" to her. It struck her as ridiculous to return to the impersonal address now, but she was suddenly desperate to reestablish distance between them.

That she had reverted to his last name wasn't lost on Burke either, Eve noted. He lifted his head and looked into her eyes, then he obligingly shifted, taking his weight off her. All the way off. He got to his feet.

Without the warmth of his body, she became aware of the chill in the air. Her teeth chattered. Burke must have heard it because he glanced around briefly then bent and retrieved his shirt from the rug. He held it out to her.

Her own nightshirt was not in sight. Eve looked about for it, then gave it up when she shivered. She took the garment from Burke with a less than graciously mumbled "thanks".

Though Burke seemed unconcerned about his own nakedness, as soon as she had his shirt in her grasp, he turned away from her, averting his gaze so she could put it on in some modicum of privacy.

Clearly, he no longer felt the intimacy of a lover.

Distance successfully reestablished.

He'd received her message, or been struck by the error they'd made, as she had, and come to his senses. Or, maybe he'd been in the mood for sex and had found a willing partner in her and that was the end of it for him.

Whatever. Good. *Good.*

But it didn't feel good.

Hands shaking, Eve donned the shirt. It was no longer warm from his body, but his scent clung faintly to the cotton. Each time she took a breath, she'd be reminded of making love with him. She didn't want to be reminded of him. As soon as she was back in her room, she would certainly change into something of her own to sleep in.

"We'd better get some sleep," Burke said.

His tone was firm. There was no mistaking "John" the tender lover with Central Intelligence

Agent Burke.

That was for the best. As it had to be ...

CHAPTER TEN

What the hell had he done?

Burke stared at the closed bedroom door, the intensity of his gaze drilling holes in the scarred wood. Eve had disappeared behind that door a moment ago.

He'd had sex with his prisoner.

He was an officer of the law. Officers of the law did not have sex with the women in their custody. But that's what he'd done. Compromised the investigation, as a result, and given Eve a weapon to use in court to have the charges against her dismissed.

He made a scoffing sound of self disgust. How could he have been so irresponsible?

How could he have allowed his personal feelings for her—he shook his head, not his feelings, his lust for her—to override his duty?

Against his will, he recalled being with Eve. Sex with her had not disappointed. Rather, it went right off the charts. Mind-blowing. The best he'd ever had.

He turned away from the door and went to the window. The wooden sill jutted out from the wall. Burke braced his hands on it.

Clouds blocked the moonlight. The darkness was thick and his own face reflected back at him in the black glass.

How he could have allowed himself to sleep with Eve no longer mattered. The question now was, what was he going to do about it?

He should remove himself from her presence and transport her to Washington immediately. Then he could get back to his original assignment, his true assignment—hunting the buyer. He was itching to rejoin Lanski and his team in the search.

Eve's assassin was still out there, however. Burke's jaw tightened. They'd made no progress identifying that bastard. Until they did ID Eve's assassin, taking her from the cabin wasn't an option.

He could call Lanski. Get another agent out here to stay with her. That would accomplish the same thing—taking himself away from her.

He dismissed the idea. His cabin was safe because it was unknown. Wasn't that why he'd brought her here in the first place? Once he disclosed her location, it would be compromised. Her safety would not be assured. No, calling in another agent was not an option. Burke gripped the windowsill with a strength that stretched the skin tight across his knuckles. He would not risk her safety.

So what would he do?

Nothing.

He would remain at the cabin. And Eve would remain at the cabin. And for whatever time they had left here together, they would stay out of each other's way.

He heard movement in the bedroom. A drawer opened then closed.

She was still awake.

He listened to her footfalls, thudding softly against the plank flooring. Her footsteps stopped. Next came a creak. The bed frame. She was now on the mattress. If her pattern held true to what he'd observed the night they'd spent at the hospital, she'd soon be asleep. And snoring softly.

He stopped a smile.

And cut off that tender thought.

* * *

He cooked breakfast before the sun was up after a restless night on the couch. Unwanted images of making love with Eve there replayed in his mind and kept sleep at bay.

He ate his meal, left the bacon and scrambled eggs he'd cooked for her on the stove for her to warm when she awoke. Next he showered and left the cabin. He needed to call Lanski and after, would find some activities outdoors to fill his time.

The sun crested the horizon. He looked up at it. Too early to call his second in command on a matter that wasn't urgent.

Burke looked around for things that needed doing about the place. He'd bought shelving for the storage shed that he'd never put up. Well, it seemed the perfect time to attend to that was at hand.

After the shelving, he worked slowly through a list of repairs he'd wanted to get done for years. At mid-morning, he called Lanski.

"Any development in finding the man after Dr. Collins?" Burke asked.

"Negative. Nothing on finding the buyer either."

"Okay. Anyone putting out the word about the formula?"

"Negative again. Our Intel has been quiet as a tomb."

Burke exhaled a frustrated breath. "Keep me apprised," he said unnecessarily then disconnected.

The day was turning out to be a scorcher. He rubbed the back of his neck where the sun baked him. He needed water.

Inside the cabin, Eve was awake and again, hunched over his laptop, though, she'd moved to the kitchen table to work. She didn't look up at his entrance.

On the way to the fridge for the water, he glimpsed the page open on the screen, and recognized it as one of the profiles on the chemist's at the conference. Yesterday, they'd downloaded the information from the agency's database onto his laptop for easy access.

His investigators had been over all of the information and dismissed its usefulness. He and Eve had gone over it all as well with the same result. Nothing would be gained by going over it again.

He thought of telling her that. False hope wouldn't help her. But then, what was the alternative—no hope? No, he would not strip her of hope. He kept his thoughts about the profiles to himself.

What he wouldn't keep silent about were the heaping plates of food that remained untouched where he'd left them.

"Why haven't you eaten?" he asked, his tone sharp.

Eve tapped a few keystrokes. Without looking up from the keyboard, she said. "Not hungry."

"You need to eat."

She looked up then. "Are you presuming to tell me how to treat my condition?"

Burke's anger flared. "Apparently, you need someone to do that. If you're on insulin, you need to eat regularly. Taking an injection and then going for a long period without food can cause a dangerous reduction in blood sugar levels."

"Oh, really. What makes you an authority on the subject?"

"I read about it."

"You read about it? When?"

What did it matter? Burke ran a hand down his face. "The night you were in the hospital. I asked the nurse for information on diabetes."

Eve blinked.

"You need to eat." His jaw tensed. "The last thing I want is for you to collapse again."

Eve straightened her spine. "Don't worry about it, Burke." She left the table, got a bottle of water for herself which she gripped in a tight fist. "Should I take ill again, this time, I'll make sure you aren't inconvenienced."

"Inconvenienced? You think I don't want to be inconvenienced?" Burke closed the distance between them. He clutched her shoulders. "You think I'm telling you to eat so you won't collapse and inconvenience me?" He reached up, framed her face gently between his palms. "I don't want anything to happen to you. The thought of anything happening to you ..." He lowered his mouth to hers.

* * *

She should end this ... stop him ... all the reasons why she should not let this go on reasserted themselves. Instead, when Burke's mouth came down on hers, Eve slid her arms around his waist. Clutching his shirt in her fists, she kissed him back.

Her head was spinning as he lifted her off the floor and into his arms. Without breaking the kiss, he carried her to the bedroom. He placed her gently on the bed then braced on an elbow above her and undid the buttons on her blouse. He moved one knee between her legs and gently stroked her. The contact made her gasp, then moan.

"Over dressed," he said.

She mumbled her agreement.

He shed his jeans, his movements jerky with impatience, then lifted her hips to remove hers. In the blink of an eye they were skin to skin below the waist and the feel of his aroused body against her ratcheted her desire.

She yanked at his T-shirt and when he'd obligingly shed that too, she splayed her hands over the broad span of his chest, then across the ridges of muscle on his abdomen.

Those taut muscles quivered beneath her touch. He groaned, pressed her against the mattress, and covered her with his big body. His mouth fused with hers and he kissed her hard as if he wanted to devour her. She clung to him, entwining her arms and legs around him.

His erection was straining against her, wanting entrance. She wanted that as well, but he drew back, ending the kiss. Before she could protest, his open mouth trailed hot and wet down her body, stimulating every nerve ending as he made his descent.

When he reached her thighs, he parted them gently then slid his hands beneath her, clutching her bottom and brought her to his mouth. The touch of his tongue on her went through her like a jolt of electricity. She threw her head back, arched off the bed, and gasped his name.

She was writhing when he finally moved over her and pushed inside her. Waves of sensation began immediately and she gripped his biceps, her nails digging into the thick muscle there.

He was as close to the edge as she was. His need as fierce. Sweat dampened his skin. His face pulled taut. As she cried out her release, he uttered a deep groan and found his own.

He was lying on top of her now. His chest was heaving as he took in big mouthfuls of air. Face down with his head touching hers, his every breath brushed her cheek. She was sucking in air as well. She closed her eyes, listening to the sounds of them breathing in tandem, all that she was capable of at the moment.

Her stomach growled.

He laughed and brushed his lips across her temple. “Let’s get you fed.”

* * *

Burke lay awake. Snuggled against him, Eve breathed deeply in sleep. After they’d eaten, they’d made love again. That became the pattern for the rest of the day and into the night. Make love. Eat. Make love. After their last bout of love making, after he’d made sure that her need for food had been again met, they’d returned to bed. He’d brought her tight against his side and with his arms around her, just watched her gently fall into sleep.

She’d been asleep for some time. As for himself, sleep eluded him. He’d made a thorough study of Eve Collins. Recalling how thorough had his body hardening again. But it wasn’t her sexy body that ruled his thoughts now. He’d studied Eve herself. Knew everything there was to know about her. And now he was questioning all he’d learned because he couldn’t reconcile the woman he’d apprehended, the woman in his bed, with the one who would create a weapon for terrorists.

Eve mumbled in her sleep. Burke turned to her. A sliver of moonlight cut diagonally across the bed. It was just enough light to illuminate her face, contorted in an expression of pain.

Burke's gut clenched. "Eve." He kept his tone soft.

Her lips moved. Her head thrashed on the pillow.

"Eve." Burke wrapped his arms around her. "Wake up, baby."

She cried out and her eyes sprang open.

"Easy. It's okay. You were dreaming. Just a dream," he said.

Must have been one hell of a dream. Her breathing was rapid. She was trembling in his arms. Burke brought her closer, pressing her face against his bare chest. His skin grew damp and he realized she was crying.

Keeping one arm around her, Burke switched on the bedside lamp. In the stark light, he saw she was chalk white. Tears still slid down her cheeks. He felt helpless in the face of her tears. Couldn't stand that something had reduced her to tears.

"Eve, what is it?"

She wrapped her arms around herself and hunched her shoulders as if trying to huddle in on herself. "I was dreaming about the accident." Her voice was strained. "About Emily."

He stroked her cheek. "Tell me about it."

She released a tremulous breath. "We were driving home from buying groceries. Emily was in the back seat. I was crossing the intersection when a truck broadsided us." Eve's breath hitched. The brunt of the impact was to the back seat. Emily was killed instantly."

Fresh tears streamed down Eve's cheeks. Sobs shook her. Burke wrapped his arms around her, drawing her as tight to him as he could, sharing her pain in the only way he could.

He held her until she stopped trembling, until her tears were spent. Gently, he raised her chin. Her eyes were red-rimmed from the torrent of tears. Her grief wrenched his heart.

"Do you dream of the accident often?"

"All the time for the first few years. Not as often anymore."

He wondered if their recent conversation about Emily had sparked the dream.

"I've been over it a million times," Eve said. "If I'd just done something differently, Emily would still be alive."

"You weren't to blame for the accident. I read the report. The truck ran a red light."

Eve nodded, but Burke believed some part of her would always blame herself.

Though the last thing he wanted to do was to bring another man into their bed, Burke wanted to know about her husband, about the man Eve had once loved. Maybe still loved. His gut clenched and his next breath came a little shaky.

He knew her husband had been the one to initiate the divorce. From his investigation, Burke had learned that she and her husband officially separated within a few months of the death of their daughter.

She was worn out, though, and he had no intention of satisfying his curiosity at her expense. His questions could wait.

He pulled back, looked into her eyes, his gaze warm and tender. He caressed her cheek, as a smile spread slowly across her lips. He returned that smile. He kissed her softly.

"Do you think you can sleep now?"

She nodded.

He switched off the lamp then rolled onto his back, bringing her with him.

Within a few moments she was asleep again. Not so for him. It would be some time before sleep came to him.

CHAPTER ELEVEN

When Eve woke, Burke was not in bed. Recalling how she'd cried all over him last night, her cheeks heated with embarrassment. He'd gotten more than the pleasure of a night of love making. No doubt he hadn't planned on her coming apart on him.

Her own ability to reveal her grief to him surprised her. She always kept her grief over Emily to herself, clutched tight to her. With Burke she'd opened up and shared her hurt. He'd been a rock for her. No matter what happened from this point on between them, she would always remember that last night he'd made the pain over Emily's death a little more bearable.

Eve left the bedroom. She spotted Burke in the kitchen. He was speaking on his cell phone. When she would have left him to finish his call while she went to shower and dress, he caught her hand.

"... send it all to me, Lanski," Burke said. His

closed the phone. His gaze fixed on her. "How are you?"

She didn't need to ask what he meant. "Okay." She smiled to illustrate her point.

He brought her hand to his lips, kissed her palm. "I'm glad." He released her.

"I'll cook breakfast this morning," she said. "Think about what you'd like while I shower and dress."

He didn't respond.

"John. John?"

"Yeah."

"Did you hear what I said? About breakfast?"

"Breakfast, right."

"Are *you* okay?"

"Fine."

Eve nodded slowly. "I'll get myself together and be right back."

He smoothed back her hair, ran his thumb across her lips. "I was hoping you'd stay as you are. You drove me crazy the other day when you showed up for breakfast straight from bed."

His eyes had darkened in a look she now recognized as passion. "I thought I'd put you off."

He made a strangled sound. "Far from it."

The thought and the appreciation in his eyes felt wonderful. She leaned in and kissed him. "I won't be long."

He nodded but she could see he'd lapsed into his own thoughts again.

* * *

He was like that for the rest of the day.

Distracted was the only way she could describe it. Whatever he had on his mind was all consuming. Was he rethinking their intimacy? Regretting?

It hadn't appeared so earlier, but the thought became a lead weight as the day progressed and he remained distant.

She turned her attention to the charge against her. She re-read the chemist profiles. Again, she found nothing in them to identify the person who'd switched her insulin.

By nine p.m., she was wrung out, emotionally and physically. Another day had ended and she was no closer to proving her innocence. Burke's cell phone had remained silent all day. Lanski hadn't called in with breaking news that would exonerate her either.

She could not despair. Not lose hope. Frustration and fear were taking a toll on her. She needed rest. Once she'd recharged, she would come up with a way to prove her innocence.

Seated across the table from her, Burke was making notes on a legal pad. He'd been at the task for some time. He looked as tired as she felt.

"Coming to bed?" she asked him.

He looked at her then. The first time in hours. "Later. You go ahead."

* * *

She drifted into a dreamless sleep, after hours passed and Burke didn't come in to bed. In the morning, when she awoke, she was still alone. She showered and dressed then found him where she'd left him last night—at the table in the kitchen.

His laptop was open, his index finger tapping the keypad. His brows were drawn together. The skin on his forehead was puckered with his frown as he read something on the screen.

A mug of coffee sat on the table. She took a sip and winced. Stone cold.

"John?"

He glanced up at her, his eyes heavy-lidded from the night without sleep.

"What are you still doing out here?" she asked.

"Tell me about Richard Patterson."

"What?"

"Tell me about Patterson."

"Why?" Her heart accelerated with a sudden thought. "Have you been going over the chemist profiles? Have you found something?" She set the mug down and glanced over his shoulder at his computer. Not the chemist profiles. The document he had open on the screen had her name on it. "What is that?"

"The Intel we gathered on Richard Patterson and you. I had Lanski send it to me."

She linked her hands in a tight grip. "Have you found something?"

"No."

Disappointment wrapped around her like a cloak.

"Tell me about Patterson," Burke repeated.

"You already asked me about Richard. On the day he died. Remember? You have a dossier on him, I'm sure. I don't know what you think I could tell you that your expert investigators haven't told you."

"You knew him. You had a line to him that we couldn't have. Did he make any new friends recently? Reconnect with an old one? Start seeing a new woman? Change clothing stores, barbers, dentists?"

He'd asked the questions in rapid-fire. Eve felt the shift from lover to agent. She'd thought they were past that. Apparently not, and the realization hurt.

She placed her arms around herself in a tight hug. "I don't know about any of that. He didn't talk about those things with me. We didn't socialize." She shook her head slowly. "Didn't spend anytime together out of the lab. We didn't have a relationship apart from the work."

"Tell me about Patterson's work?"

She lifted one shoulder. "He was brilliant. One of the best in the cosmetology business."

"According to his tax records, Patterson was doing well, but he wasn't making what one of the best in business should be making."

Burke was right about that. "Richard probably could have marketed his skill better, but he didn't have the temperament to do that." Eve rubbed her brow. "He was difficult to work with. Difficult with clients. I think the reason he took me on as a partner was so I could be the 'people' person of our firm. I spent a lot of time smoothing feathers he'd ruffled and putting out his fires."

"So Patterson had problems playing nice with others."

"I wouldn't have put it that way, but I guess you could say that."

"He had an expensive lifestyle. He spent more

than he earned. Did you know about that?"

"I know he liked nice things. I don't know the specifics."

"Did you know he was siphoning money from the business? Charging meals, plane tickets, Italian suits to the business account?"

"I knew of some."

"Only some? He'd made significant withdrawals from your bank funds recently. He was stealing from you. How could you not know that?"

Eve flung her arm out. "I didn't know it was that bad. Richard and I had gone head to head over his spending in the past. We always worked it out. In the last few months though, I noticed a change in his attitude about his work. He'd never given any project he took on less than his best. It was a point of pride with him. But he'd stopped caring. I thought he was losing interest in the business and was gathering funds to offer to buy him out."

"Why did you think he was losing interest?"

"He'd stopped coming to work. Wasn't completing projects. I don't know what to tell you except what I've been telling you all along—I don't know anything." She shook her head. "Why did you have my case files sent, John? Why now?"

Burke got to his feet. The muscles in his arms and shoulders were taut with tension. A muscle throbbed in his cheek.

He rubbed his hands down his face. "I'm going to grab a shower then shut down for a few hours."

"I—"

He was already gone.

* * *

Burke braced his hands against the shower stall and stuck his head beneath the spray. As the hot, pounding water struck him, he asked himself: Had he overlooked something in this investigation? Drawn conclusions about Eve in haste?

If so, it would be a first.

He was good at what he did. Very good. Yet, as he reviewed the information against her now, it no longer fit the way it had. Eve's guilt no longer seemed apparent.

Richard Patterson had named Eve as his accomplice. That fact was indisputable. Yet there was no reason for him to have involved her. Patterson hadn't been asked about a partner. Why had he named her at all? He'd implicated her. Why?

Did it matter except as something that Burke could latch onto to build a case in his mind that Patterson had set Eve up for some yet undetermined reason? That Eve was innocent?

Burke pressed his brow to the tile and closed his eyes. Did he want so badly to believe she was innocent that he was grasping at straws? Seeing a set up that wasn't there ...

Eve was on the porch when he emerged from the shower. She stood against a post that he suddenly noticed needed a fresh coat of paint. He'd never noticed the post looked dull until Eve was beside it.

She didn't turn when he joined her outside, but her shoulders tensed and he knew she was aware of him.

"Something is wrong with this case," he said. "That something is you. You're wrong."

She looked at him then. Her eyes were luminous with unshed tears.

"You asked why I had Lanski send the files. Why now?" Burke's voice thickened. "Because I know *you* now. I know you couldn't have had anything to do with Patterson's formula. Someone is using you as a scapegoat. We're going to find out who that is."

Her lips quivered. Tears spilled onto her cheeks.

He closed the distance between them and brought her to him in a crushing embrace.

* * *

In the aftermath of making glorious love, Eve lay with Burke's arms around her, her head on his shoulder. A light rain had started. The bedroom window was open to the screen and Eve took a deep breath of the rain smell and the scents of earth and bark and wildflowers mingled with it.

"Until that deep breath, I thought you'd fallen asleep." Burke's voice came out of the darkness.

"I'm enjoying the rain."

"Glad to hear it, but I'm getting sprayed," Burke said with a laugh. He moved his arm from around her. "I'll close the window."

"I'll do it. I want one last breath of rain-scented air."

She left the warmth of the sheet and Burke's body. The air had grown chill in the room, but Eve didn't mind. At the window she inhaled once deeply, then regretfully closed the window.

She returned to the bed. When she pressed up against him, Burke sucked in a breath.

"You're cold," he said.

But he brought her close against him. He kissed her softly, tenderly. His hand moved over her at the same unhurried pace as his lips and her body began to respond. She laughed.

"Not the reaction I was going for." Burke grinned.

"Sorry, it's not you. Five years with no sex and now I can't get enough. Amazing." She laughed again.

Burke drew back. "Five years?"

Eve's cheeks heated. She shook her head. "I didn't mean to blurt that out." She blew out a deep breath and scrambled for a change of subject. "How about those Red Sox?"

Burke frowned. "You haven't been divorced for five years."

Eve felt mortified. "No. Three, actually."

She averted her eyes from Burke but felt the weight of his stare and his implied question.

It had been so long since she'd spoken of her marriage. So much time had passed. Eve shrugged, though she was far from indifferent about the topic.

"Some couples pull together in a tragedy," she said. "When Emily died, Neil and I fell apart. We were both dealing with our grief over losing our daughter. Doing it separately. That was more my doing than his. When Emily died, a part of me died too. I lost interest in my life. That included my marriage and my husband. Neil moved out six months after Emily's death. By then, we'd been living as strangers. I hardly noticed his absence." Eve focused on the window, on the fat drops trickling down the glass. "Interest in Neil and our marriage weren't the only things I no longer cared about. Nothing in my life mattered any more. And I was angry at everyone and everything.

"After Emily died, I took several months off work. When I went back, I started making mistakes. One of them compromised an investigation. Word got around that I couldn't be trusted to do the job anymore. My boss suggested to me that I quietly resign. I was mad at the world at that point and lashing out. I refused to go away quietly. I made an allegation that I was being forced out—harassed—and went to the review board. I was hurting and I wanted to hurt someone else. My boss was a good man and didn't deserve what I brought down on him, and when it was over, of course, I had nothing to base my allegations on. I caused a scandal and was terminated. I had crashed and burned."

Burke's lips brushed her hair. "You pulled yourself out of it."

"Richard was looking for a partner to develop cosmetics. I had never considered going into that line of work but I realized that I'd had enough of death and working with the dead. I wanted to use my skill to create something for the living. Emily, like most little girls, I guess, had always wanted to wear fragrance like adult women, but the products available for children brought on her breathing problems. The first fragrance I completed was a blend of scents that she would have been able to tolerate. It was a sweet scent, designed for young girls and I named the cologne 'Emily'. We made it available to the public as a not-for-profit product so that it's inexpensive and affordable at modest income levels."

Burke drew back and tipped back her chin so their eyes met. "I think Emily would be very proud of her mom."

Eve blinked back tears and smiled. Nothing he could have said would have been better than that.

"Tell me about John Burke."

Burke fingered a strand of her hair. "I'd rather talk about you."

Eve rested her hands on his chest and gazed up at him. "How long have you worked for the CIA?"

Burke held her gaze for a moment. "Actually," he said carefully, "I work for a covert division of the CIA called the Shadow Agency."

"Shadow Agency?"

"Made up of a small team of agents I hand picked."

"What do you do?"

Burke hesitated then said quietly. "We specialize in chemical weapons terrorism."

Eve shook her head. "I had no idea chemical weapons had become such a threat."

"Most people don't. If we do our job right, they never will."

"John—"

He caressed her cheek then nuzzled her neck.

"Now, enough talk."

Eve recognized that he would say no more about his work and accepted that. The very name of his agency bespoke of secrecy. When he took her in his arms, she leaned into him. Burke kissed her as his cell phone rang. He drew out the kiss, then removed one arm from around her and retrieved the phone from the nightstand.

He glanced at the screen then announced, "Lanski. Richard Patterson's autopsy was today. I'll put Lanski on speaker." He pressed the button. "Go ahead, Lanski."

"I have the results on Richard Patterson's autopsy. Cause of death was the result of heart failure. Doc said Patterson's heart just gave out. No foul play. It would have happened anywhere."

"Okay. That's it then." Burke closed his phone and faced Eve. "We can now rule out that one of Richard's associates decided to get rid of him." His grip on the phone tightened. "Damn. I was hoping his death might give us a lead."

"We're no closer to resolving this than we were three days ago," Eve said.

They lapsed into silence. In the quiet, Eve became aware of the bedside clock, ticking.

CHAPTER TWELVE

Eve shifted in Burke's arms. He kissed her temple and tightened his hold. It was still raining lightly. Night had fallen.

"Use me," Eve said softly in the darkness.

"What?"

"Use me," she repeated. "Set me up to lure Richard's buyer."

Moonlight coming in through the curtains provided enough light to see by. Burke rose onto an elbow, looming over her. "No."

"Listen to me, John. There is no other way. We've run out of options. You said you believe I'm innocent."

He stroked her cheek with his thumb. "I *know* you're innocent." He no longer had any doubt about that.

"Then use me to prove it. Disclose my location." Her words came out in a rush. "You believe the buyer wants me out of the picture, set me up. Let him know where he can find me."

Burke shook his head. “I won’t use you as bait.”

“We have no choice.”

“Yes, we do. I will continue to hunt for the buyer.”

“Time is running out. We can’t stay here forever.”

“You’re right we can’t. My office will issue a statement that Richard Patterson is dead and a bogus statement that you were cleared of all charges. Next we’ll go through the same venues Patterson did and offer the formula for sale. The buyer wants the formula and Patterson’s accomplice wants his portion from the sale. They will both make contact.”

“That could take weeks or months.”

“You’ll be in protective custody—”

“With my life on hold. My plan—”

“Your plan demands that you execute it alone. Without me. The thought of you in danger tears me apart. I won’t put you in danger myself.” He held her face between his palms. “I won’t risk you.”

She reached up and grasped his hand at her cheek. “I’m already at risk. From our own government, I face imprisonment, at best, if Richard’s accomplice is not found. The man has covered himself so well we may never find him.”

Her voice cracked. She closed her eyes. Burke could see her bringing herself back from the edge and his heart lurched.

“I *will* find him.” Burke’s voice was harsh. “Finding the accomplice is not just a job to me, Eve.” And he was going to have to deal with that.

She opened her eyes. Tears shone in them. She pressed her face against his throat and her arm wound around his waist in a death grip. Burke held her as tightly.

"I won't risk you," he repeated.

"I'm already at risk, John. Someone wants me dead. Do you really think a statement from your office clearing me will reassure the accomplice and buyer that I'm no longer a threat? I won't be safe until they are found."

She was right. Burke closed his eyes briefly and came to a decision.

Keeping one arm around Eve, he reached on the nightstand for his phone.

"Lanski," a sleepy voice said after the fourth ring.

"It's Burke. I need you to set the wheels in motion to smoke out the buyer. Put the word out that Dr. Collins has been cleared of all charges. Send a message through the channels Patterson was using. Mimic his means of making contact. Reveal that Richard Patterson is dead but the formula is available." Burke's voice tightened. "And I want you to leak where Dr. Collin's can be found." Burke gave Lanski the location of his cabin. "Do this right away, Lanski. We're running out of time."

"Got it," Lanski said. "What about back up? How do you want to play this?"

"No back up. I'll run this one solo. We can't risk spooking this guy. We can't blow this."

"I'll get the word out immediately."

Burke ended the call and placed the phone slowly on the nightstand.

"Now we wait?" Eve asked.

Burke nodded. "Now we wait."

* * *

They were having breakfast, both moving the food around on their plates, eating little of it, when Eve heard the buzz of a boat motor drawing near. Burke heard it as well. He dropped his fork onto the plate. His chair skidded back and he crossed the room to the window in the living room.

Eve followed him. "What is it?"

"Company."

Burke swept his arm out, placing her behind him, but she'd taken in the scene outside and glimpsed the new arrival. An aluminum fishing boat was docking beside Burke's own small vessel. A man was tying a rope to a pole on the dock. Fifties. Salt and pepper hair cropped military short. The man cut the engine and climbed onto the dock.

Burke's eyes remained narrowed on the newcomer. "Stay here while I greet our guest."

* * *

Outside, Burke approached the dock and the man who stood hands on hips, eyeing the cabin in the bright sunlight. Burke's service weapon was at his back, tucked into the waist of his jeans, covered by the loose T-shirt he wore.

"Hello," Burke called out.

"Hello, there. Sorry to intrude. I didn't realize I

was short on gas when I set out this morning. I don't have enough to get back. I was hoping you might have some to spare. I'd pay you of course."

Burke nodded. "I have a spare tank in the shed."

The man stepped off the dock and extended his hand. "Ted Sanderson."

Burke clasped his hand. "John Burke."

The two men fell into step. The ground was damp from the rainfall and a slight breeze carried the scents of dirt and worms. Mud sucked Burke's shoes.

"Pretty place," Sanderson said.

"I like it. Are you staying near here?"

"No. Not much out this way. Just your place and one or two others great distances apart. Nothing for rent. I'm all the way on the other side of the lake at Salt Pines Cottages."

"You have come a distance," Burke said.

"I didn't realize just how far. Set out early this morning. Thought I'd take in some fishing. I'm not much of a fisherman. Been a military man all my life and now find myself retired." Sanderson shrugged. "The wife thought it would be a good idea if I got a hobby. Said I was driving her crazy being under foot all day. I thought I'd give fishing a try."

"How are you liking it?"

Sanderson scowled. "Not so much. I didn't have one bite and I ran out of gas."

Burke smiled at that. He reached the old wooden shed and swung the door open. Sunlight lit the interior and Burke didn't bother with the bare bulb dangling from the low roof. He bent to retrieve the can of gas he kept under a small work bench, his muscles tense. If Sanderson were going to make a move to take him out, now would be the time. But Sanderson remained outside of the shed, with his back to Burke, seemingly taking in his surroundings. He faced Burke only when Burke left the shed.

Back at Sanderson's boat, Burke filled the tank. "That should get you back."

"Appreciate it."

Sanderson took out his wallet and extracted a twenty. Burke glimpsed a drivers' license with a name that matched the one Sanderson had given him and a picture of a couple of teenagers flanking a woman about Sanderson's own age.

Sanderson took in a deep breath. "Nice and quiet here."

Burke kept his gaze on the other man. "No one around for miles."

Sanderson handed Burke the twenty then the older man got back into the boat. He untied the rope, yanked the engine cord and the motor roared to life. With a wave, Sanderson backed away from the dock.

Burke watched Sanderson until his boat was a speck on the horizon, then he turned and went back to Eve.

"Well?" She grasped his forearms.

"Appears to be nothing more than a fisherman who ran out of gas."

But as he relayed that information, he pulled his cell phone from his pocket.

"Yeah. Lanski," Burke said an instant later. "I need you to ID an Edward Sanderson." Burke recited the address on the drivers' license. "I have a print." At Eve's frown, Burke held up Sanderson's twenty. "I'll be sending you a scan of it in the next couple minutes.

* * *

"Do you think Sanderson could be the man we're looking for?" Eve asked.

Only a few minutes had passed since Burke had sent the scan of Sanderson's print to Lanski. Eve was wound tight, waiting for Lanski to call back with his findings.

"No, I don't. If he were the one, he came here to get the formula, and to take you out, he would not have left without getting his job done. I was hoping Sanderson would make a move on me in the shed. Try to neutralize me so he could get to you." Burke blew out a breath ripe with frustration. "But he didn't. I think he's just what he said."

Burke's cell phone rang. "It's Lanski," he said. He listened briefly than disconnected. "Sanderson is who he claims. Lanski ran him through our data bases. No red flags." Burke rubbed the back of his neck. "I need some air. Feel like a walk?"

Eve shook her head. "I'm going to make tea. Want a cup?"

"Too hot for tea."

Eve went to the kitchen, filled the kettle then set it on the burner. As she lit the flame, her cell phone rang. Her phone was clipped to the waistband of the jeans she wore. She hadn't had a call since this nightmare began and the ringing startled her.

Eve flipped open the phone. "Hello?"

"Eve!"

It took an instant for the harried voice to register. "Matt?"

"Eve, I know who the accomplice is. Tell me where you are and I'll come and get you."

"Matt—"

"Eve, where are you?"

"I'm with Burke. Who is the accomplice, Matt?"

"With Burke? Eve, is he near? Can he hear you?"

"No. Matt—"

"Listen to me, you have to get out of there. I will come and get you. Eve—you have to get away."

"What are you talking about?"

"The accomplice is Burke. Eve, it's Burke. I know about the bomb at the cottage. I know about the insulin switch. He's the one who's trying to kill you."

Eve had felt euphoria that Matt might have identified the man they were after. "Matt it isn't Burke."

There was a long pause. "I'm sorry, love. I wish I were wrong. But he is not the man you think he is. He's sold out to the highest bidder. He's made two attempts on your life already. He's had opportunity and he certainly has motive. Since he hasn't killed you, he must think there are too many eyes on him at the moment. His people know that you're under his protection and your death can't look like his doing. He's waiting for another chance to take you out when he won't be implicated and when he thinks the time is right, he will strike. Burke will kill you, Eve. Make no mistake about that."

Eve shivered at the chill in Matt's voice and his words.

"You have to get out of there," Matt went on. "Tell me where you are?"

Matt's urgency in learning where she was sent alarm bells ringing in her head. Could he be the accomplice? No. Of course not. He was with British Intelligence. One of the good guys, sworn to defend and protect. But how many agents sold out to the other side ...

Eve willed her voice to be calm, to stick with the plan she'd devised. Except, she didn't know exactly where she was. She certainly couldn't ask Matt to hold while she went to ask Burke. She had to improvise.

"I don't know exactly." Eve licked her lips "At a cabin in West Virginia. The nearest town is Crowley."

Matt exhaled a short breath. "I'll meet you in Crowley." She heard the click click of computer keys being struck. "There's an abandoned warehouse on the south side of town. On Little Street. Number Ten. I'll wait for you there. Come when you can. When it's safe. Wait until you're alone before leaving. Don't let Burke know that you've found him out. Don't let him suspect that you're leaving him. Bring the formula. We can't let Burke sell it. Eve, can you hear me?"

Of course he wanted the formula. Any hope

she'd had of his innocence vanished. She nodded, then realizing Matt couldn't hear her, said, "I hear you."

"I'll be waiting at the warehouse. Burke is dangerous. Eve, I implore you, don't delay too long."

"I'll be there as soon as I can." Eve ended the call and set the phone down on the counter.

He's already made two attempts on your life already.

When he thinks the time is right ... Burke will kill you, Eve.

Matt's words replayed in her mind. John was outside. Through the window in the living room, she could see him, chopping wood. He'd removed his shirt. His impressive shoulders and back, well defined with muscle, glistened. The muscles on his arms rippled as he brought the ax he held up for another swipe of the log he'd set on the ground. Could the man who'd held her in passion and in sympathy when she'd cried her eyes out over her daughter, mean her harm?

He must have felt her gaze on him because he glanced up from the log and to her. He smiled and winked at her. She could imagine the picture she made. Dressed in only his shirt which fell to her mid-thigh, her hair tousled from their latest lovemaking. Her lips swollen from his kisses and her eyes filled with the love she was feeling for him. Oh, God, did she sound like every blind, naive woman, defending the criminal she was so in love with? She exhaled a deep breath. There it was. She'd fallen in love with Burke. Like a sneak attack, her feelings had crept in. The question though remained, Was she being naive? Was she wrong?

How many agents sold out to the other side?

She'd thought that about Matt. But why not John? He was an agent, too ...

And Matt had told her at the cottage that he wanted the formula to destroy it. Had he asked her to bring it to him for that reason? Or was his request more sinister than that ...

She linked her hands together in a tight grip. Could she be so wrong about John?

The kettle whistled, startling her.

Eve blinked back tears. No. *No.* She wasn't wrong about John. She turned off the burner and went out to him.

"Hi," he said when she reached him. His gaze became scrutinizing. "You okay?"

"I just got a phone call."

He stopped in mid-swing.

"It was from Matt Deligne. He told me that he knows who the accomplice is. He says it's you."

Burke set the ax down on the ground slowly. He reached for his T-shirt on a tree stump and swiped it across his brow. "Since you're here calmly telling me about it, I don't have to ask if you believed him."

Their gazes locked. "No, you don't have to ask."

Burke nodded. "Was that all Deligne had to say?"

Eve shook her head. "He wants me to meet him. He wants to take me someplace safe away from you."

"I'll bet he does. He expects to lure you to

him." A muscle throbbed in Burke's jaw. "So he's the one. Finally this will be over." He reached out and brushed his thumb across her cheek. "I'm sorry it's Deligne. I know you considered him a friend."

Eve nodded, saddened at the realization that Matt was not a friend at all.

"Where does he want you to meet him?" Burke asked.

She told him. She glanced at her watch. "I'll get dressed and then I'd better be on my way. It's going to take me a while to find the warehouse."

"You don't need to worry about that. I'm meeting him."

"What about me?"

"You'll wait here."

"No."

"Yes."

She shook her head. "I won't sit on the sidelines like some helpless female."

Burke tipped up her chin. "You're not helpless. I respect you as a strong, capable woman. This isn't about you, Eve. It's about me. I can't finish this if I'm worried about you. I need to know you're safe. Stay here. Wait for me here. Do this for me. Please."

Eve held his gaze for a long moment, then nodded slowly.

He reached out and took her in his arms, holding her close.

Fifteen minutes later, Burke emerged from the shower, Eve sat on his bed while he dressed. He strapped on his shoulder holster, shrugged into his jacket and it was done. She followed him to the door. He turned and kissed her.

"Be careful."

He nodded.

When he was about to turn away, she latched onto the sleeve of his jacket. She was reluctant to let him go. She recalled the day at the cottage Richard had rented when she'd thought Deligne didn't take a hit well. All a ruse, she realized. Deligne was also an agent, was as well trained as John. She didn't diminish John's capabilities, but Deligne would not be an easy take-down and she was afraid for him.

She pulled him close once again.

Burke kissed her hard, then left.

* * *

Burke made good time to the warehouse. He'd considered then dismissed the notion of calling in back up. Deligne would spot an ambush.

Deligne. There would be payback for what he'd put Eve through. Badge be damned. He had to remind himself to keep from killing Deligne.

He wanted to arrive before Deligne and get into position before the other operative realized that he'd been duped and it wasn't Eve who was meeting him. Eve had not asked where Deligne was calling from. It would have been helpful to know just how far away Deligne actually was and how much time Burke had before Deligne's arrival. Lanski was monitoring Eve's cell phone. He would know about Deligne's call, but it was likely that Deligne's phone was secure as well and had masked his location. Lanski would not be able to track Deligne's location either.

Burke pulled into the warehouse parking lot. The old building had suffered a fire years back. The brick was scorched. Jagged glass remained in window frames, blown apart from an explosion that had rocked the building. There were no vehicles on the lot. It appeared that Deligne had not yet arrived.

Burke parked the car then crossed the lot to the building. The warehouse backed onto a wooded area. He took up a position among the trees to wait.

About thirty minutes later, he spotted a compact sedan pulling into the lot. The driver parked then emerged from the vehicle. Deligne.

The operative went to Burke's vehicle, peered in the windows then turned away from it and looked about the lot.

"Eve!" Deligne called out.

Burke took his weapon in hand and stepped out from the trees. He walked at a leisurely pace to Deligne. The agent's eyes widened on Burke, then narrowed and Deligne lunged at Burke.

"What have you done to her?" Deligne shouted.

Burke raised his weapon. "Easy."

Deligne stopped, but just barely, Burke thought. The agent rocked back on his heels. His body was visibly straining to leap. Blood lust raged in Deligne's eyes. The urge to kill was there.

Deligne's reaction gave Burke pause and started his heart pounding. Clearly his interest wasn't in the formula, but in Eve. Something wasn't right ...

"What have you done to Eve?" Deligne repeated.

"Eve is fine."

Deligne scoffed. "I don't believe you. My one regret is that I'll be going to my grave without having killed you for what you've done to her."

"Believe what you will, but it's the truth. Now I have a question for you. Who is your buyer for Patterson's formula?"

Deligne laughed. "Oh that's rich, mate. Turning the tables on me? Why don't you just shoot me and get it over with. Stop playing games. It's what you came here for."

Burke frowned. "Something isn't right here."

"That's the first thing we agree on. Give me your gun, Burke, and I'll make it right. I'll put a bullet in your head."

"Don't you want the formula first?"

Deligne gritted his teeth. "I don't give a damn about the formula. My country wants it. I'm of a mind to leave it with you. Let whoever finds your body take it. Let you all kill yourselves with it."

Burke's gaze narrowed further. "Why did you tell Eve that I'm Patterson's accomplice?"

Deligne crossed his arms. "Don't play me for a fool. Since she's been with you, there have been two attempts on her life. You are the only one she's been in contact with. It has to be you."

Burke rubbed his jaw as another thought came to him. "Why did you ask Eve to meet you here? Why didn't you go to her?"

Deligne gave Burke a look of pure hatred. "I would have gone to her, if she could have told me where she was. But she couldn't do that since you've gone to great lengths to keep that information from her. She thinks, no doubt, you have her in protective custody, but you've isolated her. She doesn't know that she's been abducted. Tell me Burke, how are you going to explain her death to your superiors? You going to say that you killed her when she overpowered you while attempting to escape? A big bloke like you? Do you really think that will wash, mate?"

But Burke had tuned out the latter part of Deligne's monologue, focused on one thing: Deligne hadn't known where to find Eve.

"Eve's location has been disclosed. Haven't you been monitoring your Intel?"

"Of course I have. There's been no such information. If there had been, rest assured, mate, I would have come to you, and you'd be dead."

The sincerity in Deligne's voice was impossible to mistake.

There was only one reason Deligne didn't know Eve's location. Because it hadn't been disclosed ...

"Spare me your denials, Burke. The one behind all this could only be you."

Deligne was wrong about that. Burke now knew who they were looking for and the knowledge hit him like a punch to the gut even as his lips thinned at the betrayal.

Lanski.

Burke had to warn Eve yet he couldn't reveal that Lanski was their traitor. Lanski was monitoring Eve's cell phone calls.

He considered telling Eve that Deligne was the man they were after. That it was over. He'd tell her the truth later. Would hearing that lull Lanski into a false sense of security until Burke could take him down, or ease Eve, causing her to let down her guard?

Burke couldn't take that chance.

His heart drummed as he took out his cell phone and called her. She picked up before the first ring had completed. He exhaled a deep breath, willing himself to be calm, to keep the strain from his voice.

"Eve."

Deligne's gaze darted to the cell phone.

"She's alive," he said.

Disbelief rang in Deligne's voice. Burke ignored it and focused on Eve.

"John, are you all right?"

"I'm fine. Eve, it isn't Deligne."

He heard her sharp intake of breath. Her disappointment cut him, but he couldn't allow himself to be distracted now.

"The man we're after is still at large. Stay inside. Trust no one. I'll be there as quickly as I can. Eve are you there?"

"I'm here."

"I'm on my way. This will all be over soon, Eve, I promise you." His voice throbbed with conviction.

Burke closed his phone.

Deligne shook his head. "I misjudged you, mate."

"There's a lot of that going around today."

Burke replaced his semi-automatic in his shoulder holster. He had to get to Eve. He turned away from Deligne and ran to the car.

Fifty minutes later he was back at his cabin. For the first time, he cursed the remote location and the distance from it to the nearest town.

The cabin door had a pathetic lock that he never used. Still, it was better than nothing. He'd asked Eve to lock up after him. Apparently she hadn't, though, because his key turned in the lock without resistance. He would install dead bolts at once.

Inside, he called her name. At a glance he saw that she wasn't in the living room or kitchen areas. He knocked on the bathroom door. "Eve?"

No answer. He opened the door. She wasn't there.

The bedroom door was closed. She hadn't slept well last night. He knew because she'd been in his arms all night and he'd felt the tension in her. The stress had to be getting to her. If she'd gone to rest for a bit, it was no wonder. He hoped she was in a deep sleep.

He eased the bedroom door open. He'd never gotten around to fixing a hinge that squeaked. He tried to open the door with as little noise as possible. The sound never bothered him before, but at the moment, the squeak sounded as loud as a scream. Damn. The last thing he wanted was to wake Eve.

The room caught first light, but now, in late afternoon, was dim. Even in the low light, though, he could see that Eve was not in the room. The bed was made and Eve wasn't on it.

"Eve!"

He strode into the room calling her name, a useless endeavor, since he could see she wasn't in the room.

She was not in the cabin.

He searched outside.

She was not outside either.

Eve was gone.

CHAPTER THIRTEEN

Eve, it isn't Deligne. The man we're after is still at large. This will all be over soon ... I promise you.

Eve stood clutching her phone long after Burke had ended the call. One thought echoed in her mind: The accomplice was not Matt. They were no closer to ending this, despite Burke's assurance.

She could not let this go on. She wanted her life back. And she wanted a chance to find out if that life could include Burke. He'd awakened feelings in her she'd thought dead. He'd awakened *her.* She was so in love with him. She wanted a chance to tell him that.

But she wouldn't. Would not do that to him. Not while a charge of treason hung over her head and her future was uncertain. When she declared her love, she would be free, free to explore the possibility of a life together, if that was what he wanted too. Until she was free, she would not burden him with her feelings.

The idea of spending the rest of her life in a prison, or sentenced to death was unthinkable. She could not let that happen.

She could no longer stay safe and hidden at the cabin. She needed to rejoin the world, make herself a target.

And do so without Burke's help. He would certainly not approve. He wanted her tucked away here where he could stand between her and any harm that would come to her.

Aside from his disapproval, she would not make him a party to her flight from justice. To the CIA, she would become a fugitive. She'd been a cop and a good one. It was time she took back her life. Burke had shown her where he kept his spare gun. She would—

Her cell phone rang. The number was unknown. She hoped it was the man they were after, that the plan they'd set into motion had worked. Her stomach fluttered as she answered the call.

"Listen very carefully, Dr. Collins. To do otherwise will cost Agent Burke his life."

The voice was garbled, spoken in a cold, crisp tone that raised the hair on the back of Eve's neck.

"Who are you?" Eve's grip on the phone tightened. "Is he all right?"

"I think you know I'm the one you've been wanting to meet."

Sweat trickled between Eve's shoulder blades.

"When I've finished speaking, you will leave the cabin and go into the woods. Once there, walk briskly. Keep walking. Do not stop. I will meet you. You are to do this as soon as I finish speaking. At this moment, one of my people has a rifle trained on Agent Burke's head. If you disobey my order, he will be killed. If you try to contact him, if he reaches for his cell phone, his head will explode like a melon. Do you comprehend me?"

"Ye-s." Eve's teeth chattered as she responded. "You didn't answer my question. Is Burke all right? How do I know you aren't bluffing? That you even know where he is?"

"He's at a warehouse at Ten Little Road."

Eve's insides seemed to quiver as her caller recited the address for Burke's meeting with Matt Deligne.

"You have ten minutes, Dr. Collins. Keep me waiting and Burke will be killed."

An instant later, Eve's phone was silent.

Tears welled in her eyes. They were useless and she forced them back. She wanted to retrieve Burke's spare gun from the armoire but the man who'd called her was no fool. She would not be able to keep a gun hidden from him. She would have to leave the weapon behind.

She left the cabin. She strode over the rocks and plant life that made up the forest floor. She had to make contact with her caller on time, show him that she'd followed his instructions and make sure that he didn't harm Burke.

A bird swooped up from a branch. Eve gasped. Her heart was racing and it pounded harder. Her caller had been using a device that garbled his voice. No way for her to identify him. It didn't matter now. She'd soon be face-to- face with him.

John. *John.* She picked up her pace. Fear that

her caller would make good on his threat hastened her footsteps.

In her urgency, she didn't see a rock that jutted up from the ground. Her foot caught and she fell forward, onto her hands and knees. She gasped as one palm scraped something that drew blood.

Without a glance at her injury, she pushed back the hair that had fallen across her face like a curtain. When she glanced up, it was into a familiar face.

"Mr. Lanski?"

Eve felt a surge of joy at seeing Lanski's familiar face that for an instant she didn't question his presence in the woods behind Burke's cabin. Then she noticed the semi-automatic weapon he'd trained on her. She shook her head, not wanting to believe what she was seeing about the man standing in front of her.

Lanski laughed. "No doubt you're confused. I'm quite the actor aren't I?" He laughed again, clearly proud of himself.

"All along it's been you?" Eve's voice came out weak.

"Why do you say it like that?" Lanski's mirth vanished, replaced by anger. "Don't you think I'm capable of this? Of outsmarting the mighty Burke?"

Lanski's sudden mood change sent another burst of fear through Eve.

"No one at the conference tampered with your insulin," Lanski went on. "*I* made the switch the day before when Richard died, while Burke was occupied speaking with you. *I* was Richard's accomplice. *I* contacted him about developing the formula. The plan was *mine* all along." Lanski puffed out his chest with self-importance. "All was going well until Burke found out about the chemical weapon and that Richard wasn't working alone. I covered my tracks. I don't know how Burke found out Richard had an accomplice." Lanski clenched his fists. "After that, I had to pretend to investigate. I had to protect myself and provide Burke with an accomplice. You were perfect for the role, Dr. Collins. Richard never named you. I set that up. Spoon fed it to Burke." Lanski sneered. "Once the deal was made, I intended to dispose of Richard, and you. You and Richard were meant to be my scapegoats."

"You killed Richard?"

"No." Lanski's mouth tightened. "It was heart failure, as I said. I wouldn't have killed him then. I still had use for him. I needed him to deliver the formula and to attend the meeting with the buyer. To answer any questions about the formula. Chemistry isn't my specialty." Lanski flushed at the admission. "Richard's death was inconvenient."

"And left you without the formula," Eve said.

"I set up the alternate meeting at the hotel and sent Burke the text message so I could search your cottage." Lanski smirked. "I also wanted to mess with his head. Show him that he isn't infallible. That he could be duped. And he fell for it, like a fish on the line. But the formula wasn't there." Lanski's smile slipped. "Burke thought he was so clever. We'll see if he still thinks so when this is day is done."

Eve's breathing quickened. "Is he all right?"

Lanski laughed. "All a bluff. I never had anyone ready to kill Burke. He's alive. For now. I'd love to go on telling you what fools you and Burke have been, but the thing of it is, we need to leave here now. We have more to do."

A cold sweat broke out on Eve's skin. "So many people will die if that formula is used? How can you do this?"

Lanski seized her arm. "Money. A whole lot of money. I promised this formula to the people I work for. They're not the type to accept a shrug and an apology if I don't deliver. I'll be strung up by my—shall we say, intimate parts—if I don't give them what they're paying for. I don't plan on allowing that to happen. Come on."

"You won't get away with this."

"Oh, but I will. I already have. I've been monitoring your phone calls. Another mistake the great Burke made. I overheard him tell you that Agent Deligne is the one you've been chasing." Lanski raised his head, basking in the bright sunlight. "By the time Burke learns of his mistake, it will be too late. All evidence points to you and Patterson. With Patterson now unable to refute his claim and exonerate you, you will take the wrap. You're guilty in the eyes of my superiors and my orders are to bring you in." He bared his teeth in a parody of a smile. "Too bad we won't be doing that. But, if it matters to you, you will be seeing Burke one more time when he brings me the formula. For the last time."

Again, fear for Burke asserted itself and Eve shivered. "Burke will have back up. He won't meet with you alone."

"He cannot involve the Agency. His superiors would never allow him to use the formula as a bargaining tool. He's been in the Intelligence game long enough to know that. Oh, no, he's on his own if he wants to save your life. And he knows what kind of adversary I am, so he won't doubt when I say I will kill you if he doesn't deliver. That's exactly what he will do, Dr. Collins. He will deliver the formula to me." Lanski's gaze narrowed. His features pulled taut in anger. He seized her by one shoulder and gave her a shake that knocked her teeth together. "He'll do exactly that." His voice dripped venom. "Exactly what I tell him to do. He will betray his agency and his country and hand the formula to me. And then he'll die because of it."

CHAPTER FOURTEEN

Eve was gone.

Burke looked about him, moving his head from side to side like a wild man. Had she been taken? That was the only explanation that made sense and his mouth went dry at the prospect of her being in the hands of the man who wanted her dead.

Lanski.

How could he have misjudged his second in command? Trusted him. He was trained to spot a traitor. He knew the signs. He'd missed them and now his lapse could cost Eve her life. His mouth went dry at that thought and left him as weak as a newborn colt.

Burke's cell phone rang. Caller ID read Eve. His heart thumped. But of course it wasn't Eve calling but Lanski.

"Hello, Burke."

"I want to speak with Eve."

"I'm sure you do. But you're no longer calling

the shots. From now on, you'll do as I tell you. Whatever I tell you."

"Okay." Lanski was riding high on his power. Burke played to his second in command, deliberately making his tone desperate, defeated. "You're in charge."

"You'd do well not to forget if you want to keep Eve alive."

Sweat broke out on Burke's forehead. "Let me talk with her. Please."

Lanski laughed. "Oh, I like it when you beg. Ask me again, just like that and I may grant your request."

"Please," Burke repeated.

Lanski laughed loud. An instant later, Eve was on the line.

"John—don't do—" Eve cried out.

"Eve!"

"She's still breathing. For the moment. You shouldn't have tried to undermine me, Dr. Collins. I'm going to have to teach you not to do that again."

Burke's blood chilled. He needed to change tactics, return Lanski's focus to him and away from Eve. "Lanski. Still the coward. Still hiding. Come out and face me. If you have the guts."

"Oh, I'll face you! Very soon. Make no mistake about that! You have something I want and I intend to get it."

"The formula."

"Bingo. You'll get the lady doc back alive when I get the formula."

"How do I know you won't kill her as soon as we end this call?"

"You don't. But you'll take that chance. If you don't, I'll kill her for sure."

Burke knew Lanski had him. He tried to calm his racing heart. "Where and when?"

"The warehouse where you met Deligne suits me."

"If Eve isn't at the trade or isn't in good health, I will destroy the formula before your eyes. Your associates won't take kindly to that. Hear me, Lanski. If you hurt her, I will leave you to your associates and let them mete out their justice on you. Be clear on that."

"You're in no position to issue threats, Burke."

But Burke heard a tremor in Lanski's voice and knew he'd struck a nerve.

"Two hours," Lanski said.

Burke's hand trembled as he closed his phone. If he played this wrong, Eve would die. He shut his eyes tight, battling back fear that threatened to cripple him.

One hour later, he was outside the cabin, getting ready to leave for the meet with Lanski when a boat came into view. As it neared, Burke made out a logo for a marina across the lake that rented boats and, he saw Eve, her beautiful hair blowing in the breeze.

She was alive and standing on her own two feet beside Lanski. Whatever he'd done with her, he hadn't hurt her badly enough that she couldn't stand. Burke released a deep breath of relief and wiped the sweat that had been trickling down his neck since Lanski's phone call.

Eve was wearing a trench coat. Overly large. A man's coat. As Lanski docked the boat, Burke could see that Eve stood flush against her captor. He felt a rush of fear that shook him, thinking maybe her standing upright beside Lanski was nothing more than a pose—maybe she needed Lanski to prop her up and couldn't stand unaided. As those thoughts raced through his mind, overpowering all other thoughts and emotions, Lanski stepped out of the boat onto the dock. Eve remained standing, though as Burke could now see, she was slightly bent over at the waist, as if unable to stand erect.

"Eve!"

Her gaze met his through the windshield. She didn't respond.

"Where is the formula, Burke?"

"Eve!" Burke called out.

"I asked you a question," Lanski said.

Burke focused on Lanski. "So you did." He turned to Eve again. "Eve, are you all right?"

"John."

Her voice quavered.

"Why aren't you standing upright?"

Lanski said, "She won't be standing at all if you don't—"

Burke turned his head slowly and gave Lanski the full force of his gaze. In a lethal whisper he said, "And you won't be getting what you came here for if you've hurt her."

Lanski's mouth pinched now. An angry flush stained his cheeks red.

"She can't stand because I have tied her to the steering wheel. The rope is too short for her to stand fully. She is unhurt, though."

"I'll hear it from her," Burke said. "Eve."

She nodded.

Reluctantly, he took his gaze from her and returned his attention to Lanski. “So you decided to change the meeting place.”

Lanski nodded.

“You played it down to the wire. Another minute or two and you would have arrived here after I’d already left.”

“Not down to the wire, I timed it perfectly.” Lanski sneered. “Just as this transaction is going to go perfectly. I’ve been patient, allowing you to satisfy yourself as to Dr. Collins’s condition. She’s unharmed as you can see. Oh, you’re probably thinking that since she’s okay, you can come up with a way to have both her and the formula. You underestimated me, again, Burke. She’s fine at the moment. But that could change in an instant.” Lanski reached out and snagged the coat from Eve’s shoulders.

Burke’s breath held. Strapped to her waist was a bomb.

Lanski laughed. “That’s right. You aren’t mistaken. That is a bomb on Dr. Collins.” He held up his hand, displaying a detonator. “Boom!”

Eve cried out and Lanski laughed again.

“Oops,” Lanski said. “Wouldn’t want to set off the bomb by mistake.”

Burke’s fist clenched. He longed to grab Lanski by the throat even as his own throat constricted.

“It’s rigged on a three minute timer, Burke. Surely, you can deactivate a bomb in three minutes.” Lanski snapped his fingers. “Oh, that’s right you can’t.” Lanski smirked. “*I’m* the bomb expert.”

"Here's the formula." Burke removed Richard Patterson's pages from his shirt pocket and held them aloft. "Now, give me the detonator."

Lanski tapped his index finger to his lips and scrunched up his face as if considering Burke's words. Then, he yelled, "Buzz! No! I won't be doing that just yet."

Lanski was beaming, clearly enjoying his power.

"Oh. Oh. My hand is starting to sweat, Burke. If you want to get that bomb deactivated before my finger slips to the switch, move this transfer along."

"Set the detonator on the ground now and step back from it and we'll make the trade."

"To think, after working together for three years, you don't trust me." Lanski grinned and shook his head.

"Put the detonator down, Lanski, or the deal is off."

Lanski took his gun out from beneath his jacket. "Or, I could just kill her now." Lanski pivoted on his heel and turned to Eve. He aimed the barrel of his gun at her forehead. I'm a crack shot, as you know. If you'd like a demonstration, I can send the first bullet through her ear lobe. Would you like to choose which lobe?"

Burke's heart pounded. A silence ensued as both men locked stares.

Finally, Lanski said, "I thought not. Now, you will do as *I* say. Bring me the formula." Lanski's eyes went cold. His voice lowered, became menacing. "I warn you, Burke, make a move against me and I'll blow her into the next life."

Burke forced himself not to look at Eve, to keep his attention on Lanski as he closed the distance between them. Lanski would not let them leave there alive. Lanski needed them dead to prevent them from blowing the whistle on him. He would not give up the detonator once he had the formula.

Three feet from the other man, he held out the formula. As Lanski reached out to snatch the papers from Burke's loose grasp, Burke clamped his hand around the hand that held both the gun and the detonator.

Burke raised Lanski's arm skyward as both men grappled for possession of the weapon.

"I'll kill you, Burke!" Spittle sprayed from Lanski's mouth. "I'll kill you!"

Slowly, Lanski worked the gun back down. Grunting and groaning, he aimed it at Burke's head. Eve screamed.

As Lanski was about to press the trigger, Burke exerted more pressure, his hand shaking with the effort as he turned the gun away from himself and to Lanski. It was pressed to Lanski's shoulder when it went off.

Lanski fell in a heap to the ground. Blood oozed from the wound. He was down, but conscious. The detonator was still clutched in his fist. Burke lunged for it. Lanski flicked the switch.

He sneered. "Boom!" He lost consciousness.

Burke was still holding Richard's formula in his fist. He shoved the pages into his pocket as he vaulted onto the boat. "Eve!"

"The bomb is going to blow! Go! Leave!" Tears filled her eyes. She reached out and frantically pushed him away. "Get off the boat, John! Go now!"

Burke did not respond. He focused on the bomb. The wires connecting the bomb were red, white, and blue. The irony was not lost on him. The colored wires meant nothing to him. Lanski was right. Burke did not know how to deactivate it.

"John—please, ple-ase. Just go!" Her voice broke. "Go ... "

He couldn't deactivate the bomb so he would have to remove it from Eve. He scanned the boat, looking for something he could use to cut the straps securing the bomb to her. A small tool box was stored in a side panel. Burke rummaged through the contents. Fuses. Wrench. Black tape. Wire. A knife. He seized the hilt in a white-knuckle grip. "Hold still, baby."

He blinked sweat from his eyes and cut the two straps. He dropped the knife, yanked the harness from Eve. Raising his arm high, he flung the bomb into the lake. As he pushed Eve down into the boat's hull, the bomb struck the water and exploded.

Water spurted like a geyser from the lake, spraying them. Burke picked up the knife, where it lay at his feet, and cut the rope that held her to the steering wheel. Eve fell forward into his arms.

He ran his hands over her, checking her for injury. "You're okay. You're safe." He said the words as much to assure himself as to assure her.

She was trembling, crying. Her teeth were chattering. But she was unhurt. Alive. He pressed Eve against him and wrapped his arms around her. She clutched his neck in a choke hold.

Burke crushed her against him. “I thought I was going to watch you die.” His tone was fierce.

“I thought you were going to die because of me. Why didn’t you get off the boat? Why didn’t you leave?”

He drew back. “Not without you.” He stared into her eyes. “Never without you.”

She held his gaze, her eyes swimming in tears. Her lips quivered. “Never without you,” she repeated.

He framed her face between his palms. “I love you, Eve.”

Her mouth trembled. “I love you.”

He brought his mouth to hers and kissed her hard, molding his mouth to hers. Eve clung to him and kissed him back.

CHAPTER FIFTEEN

In Eve's lab in Los Angeles, Mozart played softly on a CD set on a table while beside the CD player a white light winked on and off in a plastic jack-o-lantern. One month had passed since the day Lanski had strapped a bomb to her, put her in a boat and motored off to meet Burke. She'd thought she was going to die. But she hadn't. Burke hadn't let her die. He'd saved her life, risking his own in the process. A shiver coursed through her at the thought of how close they'd both come to losing their lives that day.

After, she'd accompanied two CIA officials to headquarters in Langley, Virginia to give her accounting of events. All charges against her were dropped and she was free to go. She'd left Langley without seeing Burke. She'd asked about him and was told that he was in debriefing.

In the last weeks she'd done a great deal of thinking. No doubt a near death experience would do that to a person and she'd come to some decisions about her life.

Eve took an empty box from the floor and as she set it down, knocked a beaker off the counter. The glass struck the floor and shattered.

Damn.

The lab door opened. That would be her assistant. The boy was a College student majoring in chemistry. He'd proven to have a good nose for blending scents. He was currently working on a blend of jasmine and hyacinth that had him very exited about the outcome. Eve wondered if he were coming to tell her he'd made the fragrance work.

She bent to attend to the mess she'd made with the beaker. Over her shoulder she called out, "Tam, would you mind grabbing the broom on your way in?"

She heard the closet door slide open. Then a man stood over her holding the broom.

Not Tam. It was Burke.

"There were three of them in the closet." He lifted the broom. "I took a chance."

Eve's heart picked up its pace. She stared up at him, not blinking, taking him in after the month-long separation.

He reached down to her, offering his hand. She placed her hand in his and rose slowly to her feet.

Her heart was pounding and emotion clogged her throat. It took a moment for her to be confident that her voice would work. She smiled. "That one will do." She took the broom from him and set it against the counter.

The instant she did, he drew her into his arms and kissed her as if he'd never let her go. She held on to him, kissing him back with equal urgency.

He drew back slightly. He looked leaner than when she'd last seen him. A little tired. Her heart stirred in sympathy.

She brushed her fingertips across his cheek. "How are you?"

"Missing you."

He kissed her again.

He stepped back, but not far, keeping his arms around her. "I thought you'd like to know that the plot has been stopped. Lanski, looking to save himself, revealed the name of the buyer for the formula. The buyer is in custody, as are the members of the terrorist cell he was affiliated with.

Eve closed her eyes briefly in relief. "That is the best news."

Burke nodded in obvious satisfaction. His cell phone rang and he snatched it out of his pocket quickly. Eve figured he was expecting the call, but when he glanced at the screen, he let the phone continue to ring.

"Dammit, Mallory, where are you?" he said softly.

Mallory. Eve recalled Burke telling her about his sister. She stroked his arm. His muscles were tensed. "John?"

"I've left a few messages for Mallory in the last week, but she hasn't called back. The last time we spoke, she told me she was going undercover. That she was working on something big." His gaze lowered to the phone he was still holding and held there, then, slowly, he returned the phone to his pocket. He pointed to the two open boxes that were side-by-side on the floor. "What's all this?"

"I've made a decision." She pushed a strand of hair behind her ear. "I'm selling the business."

"Oh?"

Eve nodded. "I want to do something more with my life." She swallowed, nervous now. "I'm hoping you'll support the direction I want to take."

He pressed her palm to his lips and kissed it. "I love you. Whatever you decide, I'm behind you."

"I want to join your team."

Burke went still then said, "My team?"

"Yes."

"If you want to get back into law enforcement—"

"No." Eve shook her head. "I want to do what I can—all I can—to stop chemical weapons from getting into the hands of terrorists."

"Eve." Burke tightened his grip on her hand. "Baby, what happened with Richard wasn't your fault. I didn't see Lanski for what he was."

"I know I'm not to blame for what Richard did. This isn't about that. Well," she shook her head, "not entirely. I can't say I would have come to this realization if not for Richard's involvement in this plot. But it's what I want, John. It feels right."

She held Burke's gaze for a long moment, then he nodded.

* * *

The next morning Eve followed Burke into a

conference room used by the Shadow Agency, the covert team of operatives specializing in chemical weapons terrorism led by Burke. The Shadow Agency headquarters was in a secure location known to only the handful of people now assembled in this room.

The other men and one woman glanced up and fell silent as she took a place at the front of the room beside Burke.

"I'd like to introduce Dr. Eve Collins," Burke said. "Eve has joined our team. Eve, meet Agents Lisa Portland, Dylan Armstrong, and Luke Falco."

Eve nodded to each agent in turn then took a seat in the remaining unoccupied chair.

Burke reached up and lowered a white board from the ceiling. "Team," he said. "We have another assignment."

TURN THE PAGE FOR A SPECIAL PREVIEW OF KAREN FENECH'S NEXT PROTECTORS NOVEL

SNOWBOUND

Coming To Paperback Soon
Available Now As An eBook

SNOWBOUND: THE PROTECTORS SERIES — Book Two

When her cover is blown in a criminal operation to apprehend a human trafficker, FBI Special Agent Mallory Burke is put in a car destined for a mountain cabin to be tortured and killed. But a snow storm results in an accident that leaves all but Mallory dead and she finds herself in the midst of the raging storm and in the care of Police Captain Gage Broderick. Mallory's relief that Gage is a cop is short lived. He has secrets of his own.

Gage is haunted by an incident in his recent past. The last thing he wants is to become embroiled in Mallory's investigation—or to feel this powerful attraction to her.

But the lives of twelve women depend on Mallory and Gage working together to stop this man—the women's lives and now Mallory's life. He knows about her. He knows where she is. And he wants her dead.

CHAPTER ONE

"So, how does it feel knowing you're taking your last ride?"

Mallory Burke didn't respond to the latest comment made by Hugo from behind the wheel of the sedan, refusing to let him bait her. He'd been doing his best to get a reaction out of her since they'd embarked on this journey into the mountains of West Virginia a few hours ago when Hugo had discovered that Mallory wasn't just the bartender his boss Billy Wilder had hired for his strip club, but an undercover federal agent.

Hugo had called Wilder with that newsflash and Billy had ordered that Mallory be brought to his mountain cabin—pronto.

Though Mallory wasn't responding to Hugo's running commentary, she was reacting all right. The gravity of her situation had her heart pounding so hard she wondered if Hugo and his companion, Miles Pratt, the other man in the car, could hear it.

Pratt, seated beside her in the back seat, turned to her and smirked. His unibrow looked like a caterpillar crawling across his forehead. His large bulk took up more than his share of the leather bench seat, wedging Mallory in tight between him and the rear passenger door. The door was locked, though with her hands tied behind her back she wouldn't be able to open it in any case. She was currently working on loosening the knot, but Hugo tied a knot with the skill of a sailor. Lucky for her, she was good at untying knots. This one was just about undone.

The knot wasn't going to be her biggest obstacle to getting away from these bozos. Problem was, when she did get away, she was going to have to escape into the snow storm raging outside her window. As she thought that, the big sedan skidded and the rear fishtailed.

"Fuckin' snow," Hugo muttered.

On this, Mallory agreed with him.

Snow or not, there was no way she was going to the cabin. She'd overheard Hugo and Miles say with no small measure of respect—and fear—that the boss himself would be there. Though she wanted to encounter their boss—Paul Considine—with a fierceness that had her pulse pounding, she wanted it to be on her terms. Not like this. Not at Considine's mercy.

Mallory swallowed hard. Hugo and Miles had been taunting her with all of the things they would do to her when they had her at the cabin. Despite her professional training and years of experience with the Bureau, she couldn't hold back a shudder at the methods of torture they'd described that were specific to her gender. There was no way she could allow these two to touch her and, she had accomplished her assignment, found out what she'd gone undercover to learn and now needed to take that information back to the Bureau. The lives of twelve young women depended on her. Mallory closed her eyes briefly. *She could not fail.*

Wind rattled her window. Mallory jerked back, nudging Miles. For once, he didn't comment. He removed his safety belt and leaned forward in his seat. Eyes narrowed, he studied the near white-out conditions. The wipers swished across the windshield at full speed, clearing snow for an instant before the glass was pelted again and covered.

"Slow down, man," Miles said.

"No way." Hugo swiped a hand across his mouth. "It'll be my head if we don't get her up there fast."

Fast seemed optimistic and foolhardy. They hadn't come across another car since Hugo had turned down this road. Apparently, others had the good sense to stay away today. Trees that lined this stretch of road swayed, buffeted by the force of the wind. Hugo's hands, inside brown leather gloves, were clamped around the steering wheel. He was trying to keep the car steady, keep it on the road, Mallory thought as the wind struck the sedan and the car veered off to the right. Just where the road was at this point was a guess. The thick snow clinging to the ground obliterated the road and it was only the line of trees that provided orientation. With the road conditions as treacherous as they were, Mallory might not have to worry about what awaited her at the cabin. She had a more immediate worry that she might not make it out of the sedan alive.

"We need to turn back," Mallory said. "We can't go on in this."

"Hear that, Miles? Little Miss Fed's got somethin' to say." Hugo met her gaze in the rearview mirror and bared his yellow teeth in a smile that made the fine hairs on the back of Mallory's neck rise. "Save your breath, sweetheart, for when we get to the cabin. You're gonna need it when you start screaming."

Mallory wanted to come back with a smart retort, but Hugo's words struck home and her mouth went dry. Work the knot. *Work the knot.* She increased the pace on the ropes to a frenzy, twisting and pulling. Perspiration trickled down her brow while she shivered with cold. Panic was setting in and she was losing it. Losing it was the surest way to get herself killed.

Mallory forced herself to stop jerking frantically on the rope. Forced herself to fight back the panic clawing at her. Directing her focus to the task at hand, she went back to working the knot.

Miles had disarmed her, but she could see her gun tucked into the waistband of his black pants. Once she freed her hands ... done!

She was panting like a racehorse. Adrenaline pumped through her. She would have one chance to grab her gun. *One chance.* She blocked out the thought of what these two would do to her if she failed.

She glanced at Miles. His attention was all on the road. His shoulders hunched as he leaned forward so he was now perched on the end of the seat, clasping the head rest of the unoccupied front passenger seat.

"Slow down, will ya! I can't see nothin' but snow!" Miles's shout was barely audible above the wind.

Mallory reached out to grab her gun. The sedan went into a spin. The world swirled crazily as the car whirled like a top. Her screams echoed with those of Miles and Hugo.

The sedan struck something—hard. Mallory was flung forward. The seat belt cut across her chest, cutting off her breath but holding her in place. In a blur of movement, Miles was thrown to the front of the car and through the windshield.

Windows shattered, peppering Mallory with

slivers of glass. She screamed. She was dressed in jeans and a parka which protected her body but her head and face were bare. She swung her arms up and hunched her shoulders in an attempt to protect herself from the spray of glass.

The sedan crumpled. The crunch of metal blended with Hugo's pain-filled shrieks and then there was silence.

She'd been holding her breath. She released it in a rush, the sudden surge pounding in her ears. She was alive. She repeated that thought and took another breath. Pain radiated from her right arm, leg and side. Her head hurt. When she lifted it from the seat back, her head swam and her vision grayed. Wind and snow blew in through the shattered windows. The cold air and wet flakes that struck her face revived her. She blinked quickly and fought back the blackness.

She wanted to get out of the car but was pinned by the front seat. The sedan had struck an outcropping of rock and the front of the car had been pushed back on impact. Miles's body was crushed. There was no doubt that he was dead. Given what she'd learned of his involvement with the twelve women, she would not regret his passing.

Mallory shifted position carefully, testing how deeply she was wedged in. Not as tightly as she feared. Keeping her movements slow, but steady, she raised her arm. She gasped at the pain that shot through her, but took heart in the fact that she was able to move her arm at all.

Gritting her teeth, she levered up on her uninjured arm to free her lower body. Her breath shallowed and perspiration broke out on her forehead as she continued the slow, arduous process of extricating herself.

She was almost completely free when her ankle caught. Again, she cried out when she forced movement, but made another attempt, then another until her foot was clear.

That slight exertion had left her panting. She bolstered her flagging energy. Her cell phone had been confiscated by Hugo before he'd tied her. There was no way to get to the phone the way he was positioned. But Miles also had a phone.

She grunted and pushed the crumpled passenger door but it would not open. Averting her face, Mallory reared back as far as she could in the cramped space and with her uninjured foot, kicked out the few shards of glass that still clung to the rear windshield then climbed out of the car. Outside, the blowing wind was deafening. Miles and Hugo had nabbed her as she'd been leaving the club that morning at the end of her shift. She'd already changed out of the mini skirt and halter top that were part of her outfit while she tended bar and had put on her parka. She was thankful for that now as the bitter cold stole her breath and burned the raw scrapes and cuts on her exposed skin.

Her ankle balked at supporting her weight and she fell back onto the wide trunk. She needed support—a cane of some kind. Looking about wildly, she saw that improvising a cane wouldn't be a problem. Thick tree limbs littered the snow covered ground and she retrieved one.

Miles had landed a few feet from the car in a

bank of snow that was red with his blood. As she crouched over the fallen man, she saw that his neck was bent at an impossible angle. He was clearly dead.

In the short time since she'd left the car, her fingers had stiffened from the cold. She flexed them and blew on them then began patting Miles down. She found his phone in an outer pocket of his jacket. Broken. Unusable. She let out a frustrated sigh. Her semi-automatic was no longer in the waistband of his trousers. Likely, it had been flung away when he was thrown from the car. She didn't like being defenseless, but she was hardly in a condition to go traipsing into the snow drifts in search of it. It was all she could do to remain vertical.

The sound of a vehicle approaching rose above the roar of the wind and then a metallic blue van came into view, glowing like a beacon amid all the white. She knew that van. It was one of Billy's from the bar. Her stomach clenched.

The driver met her gaze and his eyes widened.

Mallory's breath caught. Staying on the road was not an option. The mountains lay beyond. He couldn't pursue her into them with the van. He'd have to follow on foot and she'd have a chance.

Heart hammering, she trudged into the mountains. Her boots sank in the snow. For an instant, the tracks marked her trail but then disappeared beneath fresh snow.

The van slid to a stop. One door slammed. Then another. So there were two of them. Keep moving. *Keep moving.*

Her parka was red. The color would make it impossible for her to blend in with her surroundings. The men would spot her easily in all the white. Without breaking pace, she removed it. She wanted to turn the jacket inside out and wear it with the liner exposed but the inner lining was also red. Her long sleeved T-shirt, though, was white. She dropped the parka into the snow. She was cold and wet in an instant. The T-shirt offered little protection against the biting wind or the icy snow that soaked through the thin cotton fabric and left her shivering.

Snow crunched behind her. She glanced back. The men were giving chase, running toward her, overcoats flapping in the wind, slipping and sliding in their black loafers. The short distance she'd crossed had left her winded, but she increased her pace.

She had nothing to cut the wind that screamed like a banshee or the snow soaking her hair, her clothing and clinging to her eyelashes. She tucked her hair into her collar for what added warmth it could provide then huddled in the shirt. Particles of ice struck her exposed skin. Some of the flesh on her hands and face was cut from the spray of glass when the car windows shattered and now ice bit like tiny needles.

Another wave of dizziness struck her and she shook her head to clear it. She blinked more snow from her eyes and forced her protesting body to keep moving to increase the distance between her and her pursuers.

She glanced over her shoulder. She could not see the men now, but she could still hear them behind her. Hoping to throw them off her trail, she changed direction, moving deeper into the mountains.

She focused on putting one foot in front of the other. She didn't know how long she'd been walking when she spotted a cabin. Her side burned and each breath was becoming harder to take. Her right leg had become a dead weight, forcing her to drag it and depend more heavily on the cane. Mallory suspected the reason she wasn't feeling intense pain from her ankle was because she was knee-deep in snow and numb from that point down.

She could no longer hear her pursuers. Hadn't heard them for some time. It appeared she'd lost them. Her stomach unclenched in relief.

She could not turn back and risk running into the men and, she could not remain out here indefinitely. She needed to take shelter. She needed some time to think and she needed to find a way to communicate with the Bureau.

Her body seemed to sway toward the cabin, but she ignored the yearning. Entering a cabin could be dangerous. She winced, leery of ending up at Billy's cabin. She would need to take some time to observe the place before approaching to ascertain that the place was not Billy's.

She needed to find out if the cabin was occupied. There was a large front window, but she couldn't risk exposure from it. A window high on the front door, devoid of curtains, would give her a view of the inside.

Her vision wavered. The snow looked fluffy, untouched up here, thick and welcoming like a blanket. The urge to just lie down on that snow, to sink into it, pulled at her. She shook her head. She blinked and took another step. She had to make it. Just a few steps more.

An overhang kept the snow from falling onto the porch but the snow drift had built on one side and was as high as her thighs. Mallory waded through it toward the door, but stopped short of it, flattening herself against the cabin, letting the sturdy structure take her weight. She rose onto her toes to peer into the window. Her eyes rolled back. She fell against the door then everything went black.

If you'd like to know when the next Protectors novel is released, sign up for Karen Fenech's notification-only newsletter at her website: www.karenfenech.com

Or type this direct link into your browser: http://www.karenfenech.com/books.html

Originally Released In Hardcover

Also Now Available As An eBook

GONE

FBI Special Agent Clare Marshall was separated from her sister Beth in childhood when their mother tried to kill them. Now Clare learns that Beth lives in the small town of Farley, South Carolina, but when she goes there to reunite with Beth, Clare discovers her sister is missing and that someone in the town is responsible for her disappearance.

Clare receives an offer to help with the search from fellow FBI Special Agent Jake Sutton. The offer is too good to refuse, though that is exactly what Clare wants to do. Jake is Clare's former lover, a man she cannot forget, and who has an agenda of his own.

Now while Clare tracks her sister, someone is tracking Clare, and finding her sister may cost Clare her life.

ABOUT THE AUTHOR

PRAISE FOR THE NOVELS OF KAREN FENECH

{GONE} Karen Fenech's GONE is a real page turner front to back. You won't be able to put this one down!" —NEW YORK TIMES BESTSELLING AUTHOR KAT MARTIN

{GONE} "Karen Fenech tells a taut tale with great characters and lots of twists. This is a writer you need to read." —USA TODAY BESTSELLING AUTHOR MAUREEN CHILD

{GONE} Readers will find themselves in the grip of GONE as this riveting tale plays out. GONE is a provocative thriller filled with a roller coaster ride that carries the suspense until the last page." —DEBORAH C. JACKSON, ROMANCE REVIEWS TODAY

{BETRAYAL} "An excellent read." —DONNA M. BROWN, ROMANTIC TIMES MAGAZINE

{IMPOSTER: The Protectors Series - Book One} "IMPOSTER is romantic suspense at its best!" —USA TODAY BESTSELLING AUTHOR MAUREEN CHILD

{UNHOLY ANGELS} "... a superbly intricate tale of greed, power, and murder... a suspenseful and believable story that will keep you reading into the wee hours of the morning. Highly recommended! —BESTSELLING AUTHOR D.B. HENSON

If you'd like to know when the next novel is released, sign up for Karen Fenech's notification-only news at her website: www.karenfenech.com Or, type this direct link into your browser: http://www.karenfenech.com/books.html

Karen Fenech lives with her husband and daughter. To find out more, visit her website at: http://www.karenfenech.com